GYPPED

**Center Point
Large Print**

Also by Carol Higgins Clark and available from
Center Point Large Print:

Mobbed
Wrecked
Zapped

GYPPED

A Regan Reilly Mystery

CAROL HIGGINS CLARK

CENTER POINT LARGE PRINT
THORNDIKE, MAINE

This Center Point Large Print edition
is published in the year 2012 by arrangement with
Scribner, a division of Simon & Schuster, Inc.

The text of this Large Print edition is unabridged.
In other aspects, this book may vary
from the original edition.
Printed in the United States of America
on permanent paper.
Set in 16-point Times New Roman type.

ISBN: 978-1-61173-378-5

Library of Congress Cataloging-in-Publication Data

Clark, Carol Higgins.
Gypped : a Regan Reilly mystery / Carol Higgins Clark. — Large print
ed.
p. cm. — (Center Point large print edition)
ISBN 978-1-61173-378-5 (lib. bdg. : alk. paper)
1. Reilly, Regan (Fictitious character)—Fiction.
  2. Women private investigators—Fiction.
  3. Los Angeles (Calif.)—Fiction. 4. Large type books. I. Title.
PS3553.L278G97 2012
813′.54—dc23
                                                            2012003312

Acknowledgments

My gratitude to the following people for the part they played in Regan Reilly's latest adventure.

My editor, Roz Lippel, to whom this book is dedicated. As always, thanks for all your hard work, dedication, and support.

Associate Director of Copyediting Gypsy da Silva.

Scribner Art Director Rex Bonomelli.

Senior Production Manager Lisa Erwin.

Scribner Publishing Associate Jessica Lemp.

Designer Carla Jayne Jones.

My agent Esther Newberg.

I'd also like to thank my readers, some of whom I get to meet on book tours or in the course of everyday life. There's nothing like finding myself in a discussion about what Regan and Jack should do next! It's helpful and fun to hear your comments and suggestions. But every reader who welcomes the Reillys into their world plays a part in bringing them to life. For that I am truly grateful.

For Roz Lippel
My editor and friend
From *Fleeced* to *Jinxed* to *Wrecked* to *Gypped*
And all the others in between.
Working with you is the opposite of my titles!

GYPPED

Thursday, October 4th

1

In a claustrophobic dressing room littered with straight pins, Regan Reilly was checking her reflection in the mirror. If there was anything she hated, it was shopping for jeans. With all the boot-cut, slim, straight, bell, stonewashed, low-rise, high-rise styles, and ever changing lengths, finding a pair that fit properly was a challenge. Harsh lighting didn't exactly add to the joy of the occasion.

A deliberate pounding on the door was followed by a cheery, "It's Turquoise. Any luck yet?"

Regan glanced at the pile of jeans she'd already rejected. "I think so," she answered, trying to sound upbeat.

"What's that? You need to speak up."

Of course I do, Regan realized. "Yes, finally," she called over the thumping music that filled the air.

"Awesome! Can I take a peek?"

Oy, Regan realized. This is the part of shopping I hate the most. She didn't have to be psychic to predict the salesgirl's reaction. Regan pulled open the door.

Turquoise, not her legal name, she'd informed Regan, although Regan might have guessed, had streaks of turquoise running through her wildly layered black hair. One small section looked as if she'd been to the barber for a close shave. Another section was cascading down to her waist. The black leather halter and low-rise jeans Turquoise was sporting brought to mind the expression, "And never the twain shall meet." She quickly sized up Regan's jeans. "They're fab! Oh, I wish I were tall like you."

"5'7" isn't that tall," Regan said with a smile.

"It is to me! If I didn't wear these platform shoes," Turquoise said, pointing to her indescribable footwear, "I'd disappear into the crowd."

"Not a chance," Regan answered.

Turquoise laughed and swayed back and forth to the thumping music. "I have one more pair that you have to try on."

"That's okay," Regan began. "I think I'm done for the day."

"No, wait! I'm so psyched. I thought we were out of this style but I found one last pair in the back and it's your size! You're going to love them." Turquoise reverently unfolded the jeans in her hand and held them out. "Aren't these cool?"

Regan stared. The jeans had holes in the knees the size of bread plates. Holes surrounded by fray. "I don't think that's what I'm looking for."

Regan felt decidedly unhip. She was thirty-one years old but suddenly being around Turquoise made her feel at least a hundred.

"You never know until you try," Turquoise said with a twinkle in her heavily made-up eyes.

"That's true of a lot of things in life," Regan said, "but I'll take a pass."

"No prob. Would you like to put your purchase on your Trendsetters credit card?"

"No, thanks," Regan said quickly.

"Do you have a Trendsetters credit card?"

"No."

"Would you like to apply for one today? You'll get ten percent off."

"No, really. But thanks. I'll get changed and be right out."

"Okay. I'll meet you out front."

Regan pulled off the jeans, started to lose her balance, and stepped on one of the straight pins that she had been carefully avoiding. "Ow," she grumbled as she pressed her hand against the wall to steady herself. I've got to get out of here, she thought. She checked her foot to see if there was any blood before she slipped on the white pants that had felt chic before she set foot in the store. At the register, as Turquoise rang up the purchase, she asked for Regan's e-mail address and phone number. "You'll get advance word on Trendsetters sales!"

"I'd rather not."

"Are you sure? You might miss out on some really super deals."

It's a risk, Regan thought, but a risk I'm willing

to take. "I'm sure," she replied as she signed the credit card receipt.

Turquoise folded the jeans and placed them in a plastic bag. The words "Come back soon," had barely escaped her lips before she hurried off to greet an attractive, conservatively dressed woman in her fifties who had just come through the door.

Good luck, lady, Regan thought, as she escaped into the California sunshine and donned her sunglasses.

Regan walked along the upscale outdoor mall that was a welcome addition to the Los Angeles shopping scene. A large, modern timepiece towering over the fountain that was the centerpiece of the mall read October 4th, 4:05 P.M. The warm air and the softening of the afternoon light calmed her. And just being out of that dressing room was a relief! But Regan was ready to head back to the hotel.

Private investigator Regan Reilly had lived in Los Angeles when she met Jack Reilly, head of the NYPD Major Case Squad. The occasion? The kidnapping of Regan's father, Luke, along with his driver. Regan and Jack had worked, along with his team, on getting them back safely. The two had been together ever since. People often laughed about how convenient it was they both had the same last name, then invariably added that they looked like they were made for each other.

Regan's dark hair, blue eyes, and light skin were

termed "Black Irish." 6'2" Jack was sandy-haired, hazel-eyed, and what Regan termed "incredibly handsome." They had an apartment in Tribeca—the triangle below Canal Street—in New York City. Her parents, Nora Regan Reilly, a well-known mystery writer, and Luke, owner of three funeral homes, lived in Summit, New Jersey, where Regan had grown up. Luke loved to take the credit for introducing them. "If I hadn't been kidnapped, . . ." he'd joke, his face beaming with pride. "Anything for my daughter."

So much about my life has changed since I left L.A., Regan thought as she headed for the multistoried parking structure. It's hard to believe I was living here not so long ago. It's good to be back for a visit, especially since I'm with Jack.

They'd arrived late the night before on a last-minute trip. For the next few days Jack would be meeting with the LAPD, then they would take off in their rental car. Perhaps head north to wine country for the weekend. Perhaps south to Baja. See which way the wind blew, that was their plan.

Regan decided to stop for a moment and sit on a bench near the fountain and check her phone. The fountain that not only gushed water, but played music. Miracles will never cease, she thought as she reached in her purse. Jack had texted her. No surprise that I never heard my phone in that store. She read his message:

Looks like today's meeting will run well into the evening. Giving you a heads-up so you can make dinner plans with one of your old pals. I love you. Jack.

Regan felt a stab of disappointment. I shouldn't, she thought. His work is the reason we're here. She put her cell phone back in her purse, stood up, and once again started toward the parking lot. A slender woman wearing a long skirt and peasant blouse was a few steps ahead of Regan, moving quickly, carrying several shopping bags in each hand. A small brown bag at the top of one of them fell to the ground. Regan scooped it up, caught up to the woman, and tapped her on the shoulder.

"Excuse me," Regan said. "You just dropped this."

The woman slowed down and turned to Regan. She was wearing large sunglasses. "Huh?"

"This just fell out of one of your bags."

"Oh, thank you! That is so nice of you," she said, putting her bags on the ground. "I'm rushing too much." She took the bag from Regan, then tried to fit it in with her other purchases but there wasn't enough room. "Oh, my," she mumbled.

"If you're going to your car, I'll help you," Regan offered.

The woman shook her head vehemently as she continued to try and rearrange her bags. "Oh, no, that's okay. I can handle it."

She must be afraid I'm some kind of con artist, Regan thought with amusement. "Are you sure?"

"Yes."

"You're not going to let your old game show friend help you out?" Regan teased.

"What?" The woman quickly glanced up at Regan.

"As I recall, we had a lot of laughs the few days we spent together at the television studio in Burbank waiting our chance to wow the world on *Puzzling Words*."

The woman straightened up and screamed. "Regan?"

"Zelda!"

They hugged, then both took off their sunglasses. "I'm so sorry I didn't recognize you," Zelda stammered as she pushed back her mane of brown curls. Beads of sweat had formed on her forehead. "I'm in such a hurry."

"That's okay. It must be about seven or eight years. You look great."

"Thanks, you too! Neither of us won the big money but we both came so close!" Zelda cried. "And remember that horrible clue your celebrity gave you when you were playing for twenty grand?"

Regan laughed. "I'll never forget it."

"You were in detective school. We exchanged numbers but never got in touch."

"I called you once," Regan teased. "But I never heard back."

"You're right. My life was in such confusion. First I was so upset about not winning the money, then I thought too much time had passed to call you back."

"It's okay," Regan said.

"Is that a wedding ring you're wearing?"

"Yes. And I live in New York now. We're out here for my husband's work."

"Wonderful! I'm still looking for the right guy. Maybe I'll meet him before I turn forty. That gives me three months! But I've had a few good things happen in my life since I last saw you. . . ."

They walked to Zelda's car, during which time Regan learned that Zelda had been left $8 million by an elderly neighbor she barely knew.

"Eight million dollars!" Regan gasped.

"Can you believe it? This woman lived in my apartment building. She was a loner. I always said hello when we passed each other in the hallway, I held the door for her, and when she wasn't feeling well I offered to walk her dog. She let me do that a few times but wasn't interested in even having a cup of tea together. After she died, I was flabbergasted she left me anything, never mind that much. My building was nice, but not the kind of place where you'd imagine someone down the hall had at least eight million dollars in the bank."

"I guess it makes up for losing on the game show," Regan remarked.

"It does," Zelda said. She laughed heartily, instantly bringing Regan back to those days in the studio. Not a single bad clue went without comment. Zelda and Regan both prayed Betty White would be their celebrity partner. No such luck.

"So when did you become a multimillionaire?"

"Almost a year ago." They reached Zelda's Mercedes and loaded the bags in her trunk. "Listen, Regan, I have to hurry. This week I'm staying in an old Hollywood Hills estate. I don't think anyone has lived there in years. The owner donated the use of the house for a week, as a prize at a charity auction. I bid the most—which isn't saying much because nobody else wanted it. I'm having a dinner party tonight. Why don't you and your husband come along?"

"Jack is working."

"So come by yourself. The place is a kick. There are hiking trails next to the property. I was thinking of suggesting a moonlit walk after dinner if people are up to it."

"That sounds great, Zelda. What time?"

"8:00."

"I'll be there," Regan said as she wrote down the address. "It's so funny to run into you like this."

"It was meant to be, Regan. I truly believe that.

21

I've been studying the universe. Everything happens for a reason. I coach people on that."

"Coach people?"

"I'm a life coach. I'll tell you about it tonight. Can I give you a ride to your car?"

"No, thanks, it's up on the next level. It's easier to walk."

"Okay. See you later."

Regan waved as Zelda backed out her car. Wow, Regan thought. What a story. She turned, and immediately noticed a tall, scruffy guy wearing a baseball cap and jeans coming into the garage from one of the side stairwells, a set of keys in his hand. Anxiously, he glanced around. Regan watched as he rushed down one aisle, up the next, then tried a key in the passenger door of a small car. It didn't work. Quickly he backed away. He walked up another aisle and tried the key again with no luck.

What is he doing? Is he looking for a car to steal? Regan asked herself. Most people have at least some idea of where they parked their car. Surreptitiously Regan followed him as he went up and down the aisles looking around, then headed for the main staircase and hurried down the steps. Her heart beating fast, Regan followed after him to the lower level where he also scouted out cars. She tried to keep her distance, but when he started back toward the main stairwell he seemed to sense her presence, stopped, and glanced around. Their eyes met.

People were strolling to their cars, unaware of what was going on. I can't put anyone in danger, Regan thought as she quickly turned and started to walk away. A moment later she turned back.

He was gone.

Regan headed to the security office as fast as she could.

2

It was great to see Regan again, Zelda thought as she drove up into the Hollywood Hills with the radio blaring. If we spent any time together, we'd really become good friends. I should take a trip to New York soon. I *will* take a trip to New York soon. Zelda smiled. It's nice to have money. I still can't get used to it.

She was about to switch radio stations when the ringing of her cell phone interrupted a particularly irritating commercial for stomach upset. On the dashboard she could see that it was her father calling. Zelda pressed a button on the steering wheel.

"Hi, Dad! How's Vegas? Did you have fun last night?"

"Hello, honey," Roger Horn bellowed. "Thanks to your generosity, Bobby Jo and I are having a wonderful time."

"That's good," Zelda answered, trying to sound enthusiastic. "I wanted you to enjoy your birthday again."

After Zelda's mother died four years ago, her father had been so lonely. Friends wanted to fix him up with women but he wouldn't have any part of it. He'd have breakfast with his pals at a local coffee shop, take a two-mile walk, then sit in his mobile home up in Santa Maria reading the paper and watching television. Zelda prayed that somehow, some way, he would meet that someone special. Her prayers were answered. Three months ago he encountered Bobby Jo at a gas station. She asked him for his help with a pump she couldn't get to work. Never one to refuse, he did. Since that day she had hardly let him out of her sight.

"Be careful what you pray for" had almost become Zelda's new motto. But she was still trying to remain optimistic, and stick to "Everything happens for a reason." It wasn't easy.

"Did you win any money?" she asked brightly.

"No, but I won something much better."

"What's that?" Zelda put on her blinker and gratefully turned into the steep driveway of the Scrumps estate. There had been a lot of traffic.

"I won Bobby Jo's hand in marriage."

"What?" Zelda exclaimed as her hands went flying into the air. The car started to veer into the woods. Zelda grabbed the wheel and pressed harder on the accelerator, lurching the car forward.

"That's right, honey. Last night we were having a grand time celebrating my birthday. There we were, sipping champagne, playing the slot machines, when two rings came up on Jo Jo's machine. She turned and looked at me with those big brown eyes of hers and, just like the flirt she is, said 'I need another ring.'"

I can't take it. Zelda cringed, not wanting to hear any more.

"So I said, well, let's get you one." Roger laughed and sounded exuberant. "We're like a couple of kids. I never thought I'd feel this happy again."

Oh my God, Zelda thought, as she kept driving toward the house, barely noticing the overgrown lawn and bushes.

"Next thing you know we're grabbing a taxi, and our way to a drive-through chapel. I'm sorry you missed the wedding, honey."

Missed the wedding? Zelda wanted to shout. *It was in the back of a cab!*

"The driver was our witness. I gave him a good tip."

By now Zelda had pulled around to the back of the house, past the caterer's van. Her head was reeling. *If Bobby Jo makes him happy, I should be happy,* she tried to convince herself. *Mom must be rolling over in her grave. Mom, who was so soft spoken and sweet and understated. Bobby Jo was nothing like her. But then again, maybe that's better.*

But they only met three months ago! And it's my fault!

In July, Zelda had flown up to Santa Maria to spend the weekend with her father. A few hours after she arrived, Zelda decided to take a shower before they went out to dinner. Her father, feeling restless, went out to gas up the car. He came back with Bobby Jo.

"You don't mind, honey, if this lady joins us?" he'd asked Zelda. It was a rhetorical question. "She's on her way back to Santa Barbara from a visit to San Francisco, and boy, does she make me laugh." He'd slapped his knee.

At the time Zelda had been happy to see a sparkle in her father's eye. A sparkle she hadn't seen in what felt like forever. How could she object? That afternoon, Zelda had given him a pep talk about getting out and dating. She didn't expect him to act on it so fast.

Bobby Jo was an attractive, sturdy woman in her mid-sixties, with bleached blond hair cut close to her head. When Zelda met her, she was wearing the feminine version of a bowling shirt, if that's possible, green shorts, and sneakers. Her jewelry consisted of large hoop earrings, three different necklaces, a gold watch, and a colorful wooden bracelet. Her makeup was simple—orange lipstick.

At first Zelda had no objection to having Bobby Jo join them, even though she didn't seem like her father's type and he had met her at a gas station. But by the time the appetizers were being cleared, Zelda got the feeling that Bobby Jo wished Zelda would disappear along with the empty plates. Roger was a handsome, hearty seventy-year-old man. Zelda tried to tell herself that if Bobby Jo didn't necessarily appreciate her presence, it was understandable. If I met a guy I liked, I wouldn't want his kid with us on the first date.

But still.

And now they're married!

"Honey, let me put your stepmother on so you can congratulate her."

Zelda gagged. Stepmother!

"Hello, sweetie pie," Bobby Jo said. Her deep, throaty voice sounded like she was always about to cough.

"Well, what a surprise!" Zelda sputtered. "It's not every day your father gets married in a drive-through chapel."

Bobby Jo started to laugh. She kept laughing.

It's not that funny, Zelda thought, as she tried to fake a laugh. As a matter of fact, it's not funny at all. "Congratulations. I'm so happy for you both." She could barely get the words out.

"Thank you sooooo much. Now, I don't expect you to think of me as your mother . . ."

Have you lost your mind? Zelda wondered.

". . . but I hope we can be the best of friends. After all, we're the two people on this earth who love your father the most . . . Roger, give me a kiss . . ."

How did this happen? Zelda thought frantically as she listened to them smooch.

". . . and I promise you I'm going to take good care of him always."

"Great, Bobby Jo. I have to get going. I'm having a party tonight at the house I won at that auction." Zelda didn't expect Bobby Jo to remember. She never did. "Could you put my father on?"

"No prob. Love you lots."

Zelda shuddered. "You too," she said almost inaudibly as Bobby Jo handed her father the phone.

"I hope you're not mad at me for getting married without at least telling you first, never mind having you there."

"Of course I'm not mad," Zelda lied.

"That's good," he said softly. "Because if I thought about it too much, I might not have done it. And I'm so glad I did." He paused. "I know you want me to be happy. And one of the things that makes me happiest about getting married is that you can finally stop worrying about me. Those couple of years your Mom was so sick were tough on us. You worked so hard taking care of her. Since she died you've been fussing over me. I want you to enjoy your life."

"Uh-huh."

"It's time for you to meet someone who will love you like you should be loved. Someone who will take care of you the way you deserve to be taken care of."

Zelda's throat tightened. "Thanks, Daddy," she croaked as tears stung her eyes. "I'm happy for you. I really am."

"That's my baby girl."

"I can't wait to see you. I'll throw you a reception up in Santa Maria for all your friends. We'll start to plan it when you're back home."

"We can start planning it before then."

"Okay, but not now. I have to go. My soiree is this evening. The caterers are already here."

"What I mean is that we can make plans in person. Bobby Jo and I were thinking about driving to Los Angeles tomorrow night when the sun goes down. If you don't mind, we'll spend a couple days with you. It's not every day you get to sleep in a mansion, no matter how much it's falling apart! Bobby Jo and I are out to have fun!"

"Yeahhh," Bobby Jo yelled in the background. "Let's party! Yeahhh!"

Zelda slumped against the wheel.

3

Regan waited a moment, then raced down the stairway to the ground floor. She didn't know which way to turn. To the left meant going back into the garage, to the right was the outdoor mall. Regan went back outside, spotted an information booth, and hurried over.

A young guy, who looked properly groomed to greet the public, was chatting on the phone. He had just the right amount of gel in his hair. Regan could smell his cologne. The nametag pinned to the breast pocket of his dark blazer said Edward. Regan waved at him. He put up his hand in the "just a minute" fashion. Can't he register that I have something important to tell him? Regan wondered. Impatiently she looked around. The second chair in the booth was empty. Either budget cuts or break time, she reasoned. I'll bet the latter.

"So sorry," Edward said as he hung up the phone. "What can I help you with today?"

"I was just up in the garage," Regan said, pointing, "and I noticed a guy who was acting very suspicious. He had a set of keys in his hand and tried them in two different cars, then hurried off. I think he was looking for a car to steal."

Although Edward frowned slightly, it didn't

seem that the possibility of a criminal lurking nearby mattered much to him. "Huh," he said, unconsciously picking at the neatly trimmed fingernail on his right thumb. "I can take you over to security but my coworker isn't here right now."

"Where is security?" Regan asked quickly. He thinks I'm a nut. Shouldn't he be at all concerned?

The side door opened and his coworker stepped inside the large booth with a steaming cup of coffee. "Three more hours until I get out of here," she grunted.

Edward smiled broadly. "Perfect timing! Tara, I'll be right back."

Regan watched as Edward got up, went out the side door, and came around. She followed him into the security room on the ground floor of the garage where television screens monitored the activity on all six levels. Edward introduced her to the guard who was at his desk eating a sandwich.

The guard also seemed nonplussed by Regan's story. "People need a ticket to get out of the garage," he explained. "It would be really hard to get out of here if you don't have a ticket."

"I'm a private investigator so I guess I tend to notice suspicious behavior more than other people would," Regan said as politely as she could. "I don't think I'm overreacting. I know what I saw. Would you like a description of the guy?"

"Why not?" He pulled open a drawer and fished around for a pen.

When Regan left, she shook her head. Neither Edward's nor the guard's reaction made sense. What good would it do them if this mall got a reputation for car theft? Shoppers would go elsewhere. They'd be out of a job, that's what. No one would come here.

Back at her car, Regan unlocked the door. Once inside, she replied to Jack's text and told him about her plans for the evening. She didn't mention what had just happened. No use worrying him.

On her way back to the Island Hotel, a luxurious new establishment near Rodeo Drive in Beverly Hills, Regan finally smiled. Wait until Jack hears about my afternoon, she thought. I think he'll agree with me that guy was probably looking for a car to steal. He'll tease me about my jeans. But for now I'm sure he's glad that I have something to do tonight.

At the hotel, Regan left the rental car with the valet. Staff members greeted her as she made her way to the spacious gleaming marble lobby and walked past a cocktail lounge where the after-work drinks crowd was starting to gather. When she reached her room on the sixth floor, Regan dropped her purse and shopping bag, kicked off her shoes, and poured herself a glass of water from the bottle on the nightstand. The pale apricot carpeting and draperies were soothing. The soundproofed room was calm and quiet. It was a world apart from that dressing room.

Regan sipped the water. I could get used to living in a hotel like this for at least a little while, she thought. It's not bad going out, leaving an unmade bed and a breakfast tray, and coming back to find everything spotless.

I should feel more relaxed, but I know why I'm not.

Regan went over to the desk, turned on her laptop, and started to research auto theft. One headline that struck Regan's eye said that the most car thefts occur on New Year's Day. After a night of merriment, people call cabs. When they return after sleeping it off, their beloved set of wheels is nowhere to be found. Make that the second headache of the day. Any New Year's resolution to think positive is down the drain.

Regan scrolled down the page. Car thieves must hate it when big snowstorms hit on New Year's Eve. Cuts into the business when people stay home.

Why can't I get that guy out of my head?

Regan glanced at a few more articles. A lot of what she read she already knew. The most luxurious cars are not usually targeted. Mid-priced popular cars are stolen for their parts. These days car tracking devices can help, but only when drivers quickly realize that their car is gone. If your car is stolen when you are just settling in with your popcorn to watch a three-hour movie, good luck. By the time the credits roll, the only part you might retrieve is the glove compartment.

Oh well, Regan thought. There's nothing I can do about it now. I gave security my cell phone number. If at the end of the day a car is missing, they can call me. I'm pretty sure I can identify the guy.

Regan got up, went over to the bed, and pulled back the spread. She folded it up and placed it on the chaise lounge. I'll just rest for a few minutes, she thought, then get up and take a shower. With the three-hour time difference I don't want to be too tired at Zelda's party.

She went into the bathroom and changed into a white terrycloth bathrobe with the hotel's insignia. When she returned to the bed she laid down, not expecting to actually fall asleep. But she did. The soothing room did its job.

But it couldn't protect her from her dreams.

She dreamed she was in the dark, running away from someone, but she didn't know where she was.

And there was no sign of Jack.

4

Zelda rushed to the back door of the house, her mind a blur, her hands full of shopping bags. I can't believe that Dad and Bobby Jo are coming here! They could have given me a little time to absorb the fact that they're united in holy wedlock before I lay eyes on them again. In another day they'll be showing up on my doorstep, except it isn't my doorstep. I have clients coming to the house. Once they get a load of Bobby Jo, they'll never want to take advice from me again.

Placing the bags on the ground, Zelda ran back to the car to collect the rest of her purchases. After gathering the packages Regan had carried for her, she slammed the trunk shut. Wait 'til Regan hears this! I just know she'll understand. I'm quite sure she hasn't gone through anything similar, but I remember we talked about being only children. You get all the attention but it also means you don't have anyone who's in the same boat. If it sinks, you're all alone. And I feel like I'm sinking.

Zelda hurried to the back door, pushed it open, and stepped inside the big, long kitchen. The pink appliances from the 1950s that had seemed like a kick before she left for the mall, now appeared to be just what they were—old and decrepit.

Nothing like a crisis to force cold broad daylight into your brain.

Suddenly an impatient Zelda had a lot of questions. Who are the owners of this place anyway? Who are the Scrumps? If they don't live here, and they're not taking care of the place, why don't they sell it? It's a nice piece of property not far from a hiking trail. At the right price I'm sure someone would take it off their hands. New owners would most likely tear the house down and build a home with running water that you didn't have to let flow forever before getting rid of the rust. Which reminds me. I should go upstairs and turn on the faucet to the tub. I really need to soak and calm down before my guests arrive.

Another question—where are the caterers? Trays of hors d'oeuvres were lined up on the table. Even the sight of pigs in a blanket didn't cheer her. Cartons of food and cases of wine covered most of the yellowed linoleum, which was a good thing. Where is everybody? she wondered. But she had an inkling.

She walked across the creaky kitchen floor, tiptoed down the hallway, and took a quick peek around the corner. At the other end of the vast living room, standing in front of a grand fireplace, and below a portrait of a flapper doing the jitterbug, her assistant Norman was lecturing four people seated in folding chairs. Oh Norman, Zelda thought, lighten up. Lately it seemed that whenever he was dealing with people on her behalf, he became overbearing and did more harm than good. What's with that? Here I am, a personal coach, trying to help people feel better about themselves, which in turn is supposed to make the world a better place, and I've got an aggravating assistant!

Them's the breaks, Zelda told herself, as she turned away and took a back staircase up to her bedroom. At the moment I've got more important things to worry about.

"We have to make sure everything is perfect," Norman repeated for the fourth time as he adjusted his bow tie and pushed back his horn-rimmed glasses. "Perfect perfect perfect." He patted the back of his receding blond hair, as if to make sure it was still there.

Since Zelda had received her unexpected windfall, the slim, slight, thirty-three-year old Norman had helped manage her life. He'd lived down the hall from Zelda in her old apartment building, and now often lay awake at night pondering his bad luck. There was no way he'd ever have offered to walk their elderly neighbor's dog. The mutt had come bounding down the hall the day Norman moved in, and lifted his leg over a bag of Norman's groceries. From that moment on, Norman ran away when he saw the dog, or his master, heading in his direction. Ran away from a fortune. Now Norman could often be seen in his neighborhood walking three or four dogs at once. Free of charge. Their owners were all senior citizens.

Norman liked working for Zelda. But he wanted to find his own career. He had secretly started taking singing lessons after someone complimented his performance at a karaoke bar. His instructor told him he had a good voice, real potential, but he wondered if she said that to keep him coming back week in and week out. He cleared his throat unconsciously. "Don't forget, always be polite to the guests, no matter how annoying they might seem. Polite but detached. Don't engage in much chitchat. Remain unobtrusive while you do your job. After the hors d'oeuvres are passed, we'll start the buffet, then coffee and dessert will be served. It will be a lovely party. Just what Miss Zelda wants."

His captive audience consisted of two young men and two young women, all aspiring actors. They were relying on their training to act interested. The boss was telling them what they already knew.

Maggie, a character actress who had worked at numerous parties all over Los Angeles, could barely keep from groaning. *Miss* Zelda? she thought with disgust. Give me a break. It's going to be a long night. I've only been here ten minutes and this nerd in his tweed jacket and dorky shoes is already getting on my nerves. And what's with this place? The bright red living room was probably grand in its day but needs a lift. Like what everyone in Hollywood over the age of twelve gives their face. No wonder the owners of this house donated it to charity for a week. They'll take a writeoff for their generousity, claiming the rental would have been worth a good twenty grand. What a racket.

"Any questions?" Norman asked. "Any anything?"

Maggie raised her hand. "The sorbet must be melting by now," she said in a stage whisper, pointing to the kitchen.

Norman flinched. "We wouldn't want to have that happen now, would we?"

"No," Maggie answered solemnly as her fellow waiters looked at her with amusement. "We want everything to be perfect."

"Shall we, then?" Norman sniffed. "But first I'd like you all to sign confidentiality forms."

Maggie almost burst out laughing. Now I've heard everything, she mused. I don't get the feeling we'll be serving the crowd you see at the Oscars. This guy is delusional! I can't wait to talk to the others about this. A sudden thought gave Maggie pause.

But if he's not delusional, what is he hiding?

5

Regan awoke with a start, breathing hard. For a moment she didn't know where she was. Then she realized—the hotel in Beverly Hills. Thank God, she thought. That dream was crazy.

The clock next to the bed read 6:15.

Regan got up and headed for the shower, feeling oddly unsettled. She always appreciated Jack, but at times like this she appreciated him even more. If he were here I'd be fine. I can't wait to see him later.

There were four different light switches for the spacious bathroom. Regan played with the dimmers until she found the right setting. This bathroom is unbelievable, she thought, admiring the marble flecked with tones of apricot, white, and beige. There were two sinks and lots of counter space, a large bathtub, a separate shower stall, and a toilet behind a closed door.

It's so civilized, Regan thought. And it sure beats the outhouse at camp. What made me think of that? Suddenly Regan turned and went to the door of the room, pressed the DO NOT DISTURB button next to it, and secured the chain. That should keep the bogeyman away, Regan said to herself, remembering the scary stories she and her fellow campers told each other late at night, tucked in their sleeping bags, freezing to death. After three days of roughing it, ten-year-old Regan couldn't wait to get home. She'd had enough of campfire stew, watered down fruit drink, and bug bomb spray.

Even though Regan had already used the shower, she still had trouble figuring out which faucet was connected to which spray. There were nozzles everywhere. After a few minutes of trial and error, the water felt great. By 7:30 Regan was dressed and ready to leave. She'd chosen a pair of black dressy pants, a silk top, and high-heeled sandals.

She'd called for the car. When she got downstairs, the valet was pulling it into the driveway. He opened the driver's door, and wished her a good night as she handed him a tip. Here we go, Regan thought, as she buckled her seat belt, then programmed the address into the GPS. Twenty-five minutes later she was turning into the driveway of the Scrumps mansion.

She didn't know that she'd been followed.

6

In a small house set back from a rural road forty miles north of Los Angeles, Clarence and Petunia Hedges sat down to dinner. Both in their mid-fifties, they'd been married for thirty years. The first night they laid eyes on each other at a singles bar in San Diego, they knew they were made for each other. It takes one to know one. People with no moral compass, that is.

Petunia, a statuesque woman with blond highlighted hair, and a voice that on occasion tended toward grating, favored black stretch pants and boots and colorful tops. She wore big earrings and lots of jewelry.

"Pass the fries," Clarence grunted, his eyes glued to the large television screen on the wall.

"They're closer to your plate than mine," Petunia remarked as she pushed the dish sideways until it grazed his hefty forearm. She picked up a bottle of ketchup, and started to do battle with it. "You didn't want a vegetable, did you?"

Clarence knew better than to say yes. He shook his head, taking a bite of meat loaf. A big burly guy, his reddish hair was parted in a perfectly straight line, and combed into a style befitting an altar boy. "Fries are enough of a vegetable for me. What's for dessert?" His eyes never left the TV screen.

"Cake from a box."

Clarence started clapping wildly. "Yes!" he cried, raising his arms in the air. "Way to go!" One of the San Francisco Giants had hit a home run.

Petunia rolled her eyes. The last time they had a romantic dinner was before cell phones were invented. But she was happy. Happy but restless to make more money.

Out in public this twosome gave the impression of being your average middle-aged couple. Clarence drove a truck, Petunia was a manicurist. They had raised their children in a San Diego suburb, and had moved north after their youngest graduated from college. With the kids gone, the time was ripe for Petunia to put her schemes in motion, far away from her nosy old neighbors. She had rented a PO box in a large post office half an hour away from their new home, and hoped that all the packages she received would not raise suspicions.

Working in the nail salon as a manicurist, Pet loved to listen to her clients' problems, all the while honing her vast knowledge of the weaknesses of the human condition. Weaknesses she could seize upon. Tsk tsking, she applied polish with the precise skills of a surgeon, peppering the conversation with her standard remarks. "Such a shame." "It's just not right."

"Who needs a friend like that?" "I can tell you're special." "Someone like you deserves much better."

She always got a good tip.

The best customers were the men and women from out of town. They didn't worry about what they told Petunia because they figured they'd never see her again. Hint to those customers—the world keeps getting smaller.

"You should be a shrink," a New Yorker said admiringly just this afternoon. "I've never told a stranger so much personal information."

Petunia sighed contentedly. "I'd never make it through medical school. I was born to do people's nails and listen to their problems at the same time. I'm so grateful I found my calling."

Cha ching!

Finally a commercial came on. Clarence turned his attention to his plate. "So how was your day?"

"Good. I went to the post office after work."

"Yeah."

"And I got a lot of great stuff from celebrities for the 'fundraiser.'" She laughed. "If they only knew the fruits of their labor were going up on the Internet for sale. I'm telling you, I worked hard on that letter! And it looked so official."

Clarence sipped his beer. "What kind of stuff did you get?"

"CDs, signed photos, books. Some of the celebrities wrote little notes wishing me luck and saying how wonderful I am for taking the time to raise money for needy children."

"Oh, brother," Clarence said. "Not that I care, but I look at it this way. It makes them feel good to think they're donating for a worthy cause. Let's leave it at that. Because it is a worthy cause!"

They both laughed and clinked their drinks. "To a worthy cause," they said at the same time.

Petunia sipped her wine. "One thing I might keep for myself is a signed book from the author Nora Regan Reilly. No matter what, I definitely want to read it first."

Clarence wasn't listening. The commercial was over and the game was back on. "LET'S GO SAN FRANCISCO!" he bellowed. "LET'S GOOOO!"

7

Approaching the top of Zelda's driveway, Regan could see that it looped into a wide circle on the side of the house. A valet signaled her to pull forward. When she reached him, she rolled down the window. "Not much room for parking, huh?"

"That's why I'm here. We're parking the cars on the street."

"Oh. I didn't see any out there."

"We're taking the first cars all the way down to the dead end while we have the time. In twenty minutes people will all be arriving all at once. We save the spaces nearer the house for those cars so we don't keep people waiting as long."

"Makes sense," Regan said, putting the car into drive and securing the emergency brake. "How far down does the road go?"

"Maybe a quarter of a mile."

"It looks like nothing but woods ahead. Are there are any other houses?"

"No, ma'am, no houses. You're right about the woods. There's a hiking trail just past the dead end. It's a nice one. But people don't really start their hikes there because the town has strict rules about parking on this street. We've got a permit for tonight."

"I see," Regan said, accepting the claim check. "Thanks."

"You bet."

As Regan followed the path that led to the front door, the valet drove her car down the driveway and turned left, then seemed to disappear. The woods beyond the lawn were thick and dark, blocking any view of the road.

Bright outside lights on the house illuminated the wild lawn and bushes. This place is certainly interesting, Regan thought. It's obviously been here for years. And looks like it hasn't changed much. I wonder what the parties in this house were like when it was first built. Was it a Hollywood scene? Now it looks as if it's inhabited by ghosts.

She rang the bell.

A moment later Zelda opened a large, creaky front door. "Regan!"

"Zelda, great to see you."

"Come on in!"

"Well, don't you look like quite the hostess," Regan noted as she stepped inside and pointed to Zelda's floor-length black skirt, and low-cut red top. Zelda's hair was pulled up, decorated with rhinestone hairpins. "You're so festive."

"Thanks. And you look fantastic. I'm so glad you're here. Take off your coat. I want you to meet a couple from my old building before it gets too crowded."

A young woman appeared and took Regan's jacket. Regan smiled, then followed Zelda into the living room. The lights were low; candles were glowing. Soft music was playing on a stereo. Two men were sipping drinks, staring up at a portrait of a flapper.

"Curtis, Blair, say hello to my friend Regan Reilly."

The men turned and greeted her. Curtis was tall with a short light brown beard and an earring in his left ear. Bald, and a bit rounder, Blair was of average height. They were both wearing jackets and well pressed designer jeans.

"Nice to meet you," Regan said.

"Regan and I were on a game show together, years ago," Zelda said excitedly. "I can't believe I ran into her today after all these years!"

"A game show?" Curtis asked incredulously. "Stop it!"

"Yes!" Zelda answered. "Can you believe it? Regan and I bonded during a very stressful situation."

"Stressful?" Curtis gathered peanuts from a bowl on a side table and started to laugh.

"Of course it was stressful!" Zelda protested. "Who wants to make an idiot out of herself on national television?"

"Honey, that's why I'd never go on *Jeopardy*. Never!" Curtis insisted. "With my luck all the categories would be about football."

Blair affectionately put his hand on Curtis's shoulder. He shook his head and guffawed. "Can you imagine?"

Regan laughed. "Well Zelda and I didn't do so well on *Puzzling Words.*"

"Zelda's payday was in her own backyard," Blair remarked playfully, rolling his eyes. "We have an apartment on the floor above where Zelda lived when she struck it rich." He turned to Curtis. "I knew we should have gotten the apartment downstairs. But would I have done something nice for that cranky old lady? Probably not."

"Hey, hey, hey," Zelda said with a smile. "She was misunderstood."

"Join the club," Blair retorted.

Zelda turned to Regan. "These guys moved into my building a couple years after we were on that show."

"Here comes another neighbor," Curtis pronounced.

"Norman, come over and meet my friend Regan."

They were introduced, and Zelda filled Regan in on Norman's background. "We're friends and now he's working for me. He's staying here with me this week. It's fun to share this crazy place."

"If you think we're kicking ourselves about the money," Blair said wickedly, "Norman is never going to get over it. He lived two doors down from Mrs. Moneybags."

They were all amused, including Norman, although he didn't seem to find it as funny as the others.

"I couldn't stand her dog," he said.

"Whatever happened to the dog?" Regan asked.

"He was very old and died a few weeks after the woman did," Zelda said. "It was sad, but I think the dog's heart was broken."

"No more than Norman's," Curtis chuckled.

"That is sad," Regan agreed. "Dogs get so attached to their owners." She paused, then tried to lighten the air. "Well, if someone had to inherit the money, aren't you glad it was your friend Zelda?"

Norman looked at Regan. "We're thrilled for Zelda. But if we'd paid attention to her and helped her out. . . ."

Zelda put her hand on Norman's elbow. "Let's just have fun."

Thankfully the doorbell rang. A group of men and women from Zelda's yoga class all arrived at the same time.

"You didn't all ride together?" Zelda asked, her eyes twinkling.

Kevin, the yoga teacher, answered, "Carmen has a seven-seat SUV." He put his arm around a woman with long black hair. "She's our designated driver. Right, Carmen?"

Carmen nodded. "Next time, you drive!"

"Well, come on in," Zelda urged them, ever the

gracious hostess. She was working hard to make sure her guests felt welcome and had a good time.

Zelda introduced Regan to a young man who was getting his start directing horror movies. "Hey, Zelda, how long are you going to be living in this place? I want to film my next movie here."

A variety of delicious hors d'oeuvres was passed. The conversation flowed. Zelda kept pulling Regan aside to meet new people.

"Regan, this is Rich Willowwood."

"Hi, Rich." Regan extended her hand to a young man with light brown hair who was wearing a suit.

The doorbell rang again. "Excuse me," Zelda said, and hurried off.

"Hello," Rich answered, looking bewildered. He was basically nondescript, and didn't have the colorful personality that so many of Zelda's other friends had.

He must be shy, Regan thought. He's certainly more conservative than the rest of the crowd. She explained how she knew Zelda. "And you?" she asked.

"I'm her financial adviser," he answered, grabbing a glass of champagne from a passing waiter.

"Oh," Regan said. "Zelda obviously needs one."

A young woman approached them and looked at Regan uneasily.

"This is my girlfriend Heather," Rich said, his expression brightening.

Heather looked as nondescript as Rich. They could have been twins. She was wearing a plain gray dress, nude-colored stockings, and sensible black shoes.

"Hello, Heather," Regan said, trying to put her at ease. I have no interest in your boyfriend, she thought, making sure her left hand with her wedding ring was visible. "Isn't this a nice party?"

Heather nodded. "Yes."

"Do you live around here?" Regan asked, struggling to make conversation.

"I live in Burbank, and Rich lives in Santa Monica," Heather said, gazing at Rich. They smiled at each other in a sweet, old-fashioned way.

Well, that's good, Regan thought. They don't look like the type who will take Zelda's money and head to the gambling tables at Vegas. After a few minutes Zelda came by and introduced "Gladys the bookkeeper."

The petite, white-haired seventyish Gladys giggled. "Zelda, I do other things in life, you know."

Zelda's eyes shone. "I know, Gladys. A lot more. You're my surrogate grandmother. Boy, do I have a tale to tell you all." She paused. "I was going to wait but I may as well tell you now. Last night my father married that woman in Vegas!"

"Oh no!" Rich, Heather, and Gladys exclaimed at once.

Regan waited for the explanation. It didn't take long.

Zelda looked at Regan. "My mother died a few years after we were on the game show. My father met this woman three months ago. I want him to be happy, but she's not what I expected he'd end up with."

Gladys looked pained. "You poor dear." She patted Zelda's hand. "We'll talk about it."

Regan thought she detected a slight tearing in Zelda's eyes but it vanished as quickly as it came. Zelda didn't want to ruin her party.

Dinner was served, then dessert. Finally, as often happens at such occasions, two or three guests start to say good night and others quickly follow. Regan found her purse and checked her phone. Jack had texted that he wouldn't be back until at least midnight. It was 10:45. She slipped down the hallway to retrieve her coat.

Gladys was coming out of the coat room, followed by Heather and Rich. "Oh my, it's like they're speaking a different language than we are," she laughed, as she put a scarf around her shoulders. "Good night, Regan. It was lovely to meet you."

"You too."

When Regan came back out to the living room, Zelda was standing at the front door.

"Thank you, Zelda," Regan began.

"Oh Regan, can you stay a few extra minutes and have a cup of tea with me?"

"Sure, Zelda," Regan answered, suddenly

feeling concerned. Zelda didn't look well. The color had drained from her face. She must be more upset about her father's marriage than she was letting on.

After the last guest left, they went into the living room and sat on the couch. One of the waiters placed a tray of tea and cookies on the coffee table. A flustered Norman, who'd been supervising the cleanup, hurried into the room.

"Zelda, everything is put away. The kitchen is cleaner than it's been in fifty years. The caterers did a wonderful job."

"That's great, Norman. You've worked hard. Join us for tea, or if you're too tired, just go upstairs and relax."

"I can never relax," Norman said, only half joking. "Zelda, one of the elderly women in the neighborhood whose dog I walk occasionally just called. She's in her pajamas watching a special and her dog wants to go out. That's what I get for trying to plan for my retirement!! If I run down, walk the dog, and run back, I shall return within the hour. Is that okay?"

"Norman, just sleep in your own bed tonight. I'll be fine."

"Are you sure?" he asked, waving his hand.

"Yes, I'm sure. Don't worry. The party was wonderful."

Five minutes later, the caterers and Norman were gone.

"Now you can hear the tick of that grandfather clock," Regan said, thinking she'd hate to stay in the house alone. It felt so isolated, as if they were far away from the rest of the world.

"Yes," Zelda said weakly, sipping her tea.

They started to chat, but Zelda had lost all her pep.

"I should let you get to bed," Regan said. "You look so tired."

"I don't know why I don't feel well. I only had one glass of wine. This came on all of a sudden." Zelda's eyes looked glassy. Her head started to slump.

"Zelda, are you all right?" Regan asked quickly.

"I think I'm going to be sick." Zelda got up and headed to the bathroom as fast as she could.

Regan waited outside the door. A few minutes later, Zelda came out. She was as white as a ghost. "Where is your bedroom?" Regan asked.

"Upstairs."

Regan led her up the staircase and into her room. Zelda ran into the master bathroom and got sick again.

"Zelda, do you want me to call a doctor?"

"No, don't be silly. I've got a bug, that's all."

Regan helped Zelda out of her clothes and into a nightgown, then got her into bed.

"I'm okay, Regan, you can go," Zelda said, her voice weak.

"Absolutely not. You're too sick. I'm not going to leave you by yourself. If you get sick again. . . ."

Zelda's eyes were closed. Her forehead was beaded with sweat. Regan went to the bathroom and came back with a cold washcloth.

"Thank you."

Regan sat in a club chair next to the bed. I can't leave her, she thought. Zelda might need a doctor.

And besides that, something tells me she should not be left alone. Regan looked around the vast, creepy bedroom. Especially in a place like this.

8

The dinner Jack attended in downtown Los Angeles, presided over by the commissioner of the LAPD, ended at 11:15. They would reconvene at police headquarters at 8:00 the next morning. A driver was taking Jack back to his hotel in Beverly Hills and would then drop off a ranking officer from the San Francisco Police Department at his relatives' home in Century City. While they were walking to the car, Jack checked his cell phone. Regan had texted him.

> I'm still at my friend Zelda's house. She got sick and I'm the last one here. Don't think I should leave her. Call when you can. Love, Regan

Jack sighed. It had been a long day and he was looking forward to being with her. But it's just like Regan to take care of someone she barely knows. That's one of the reasons I love her. I'll wait until I get back to the hotel to call.

Jack and his colleague exchanged small talk in the car, mostly about the upcoming World Series.

"I think the Yankees will go all the way," Jack predicted.

"No, they won't. San Francisco has the right stuff!" the officer countered.

Jack was dropped off first. When he stepped into the hotel lobby, he couldn't help but hope that circumstances had changed and Regan would be upstairs waiting for him. But when he unlocked the door to their room and pushed it open, he knew she wasn't there. The door wasn't bolted—which she would have been sure to do if she were alone in the room this late—and the room was still except for the sound of soft classical music. Turn-down service, he thought. They take off the spread and fold it, refresh the towels, and turn on the clock radio set to a station that plays Mozart.

Does anyone keep the radio on in a hotel room? he wondered as he let the door close behind him. He walked past the bathroom, went around the foot of the bed, and shut off the music. He smiled, thinking of what Regan might say.

"What? Don't you got any culture? Hah?"

He sat on the bed and pulled out his phone. The call to Regan went straight to voice mail. After the beep, he said, "Sweetie, it's me. I'm back at the hotel. Give me a call. I want to make sure everything's okay. Do you want me to come join you? Wherever you are? Okay. Love you." He hung up, then texted her as well.

A moment later she called back, sounding a little anxious. "Jack, the phone service up here is spotty. My phone didn't even ring. It went straight to voice mail."

"That's okay. What's going on?"

Regan related the events of the evening. "Right now I'm by the front door. At least my phone works down here. I don't want to leave Zelda alone overnight. She got violently ill and is so weak. If she got up to go to the bathroom again, she could fall."

"Is she sleeping?"

"Fitfully."

"You don't want to call that assistant and ask him to come back?"

"I feel a little bit mean leaving Zelda."

"At least call and ask if she has any medical conditions you should know about. I'm serious."

"You're right. But I don't know his number. I'll see if I can find it around here."

"Take a look and call me back. I could take a cab up there. I don't like the thought of you in some strange place up in the Hollywood Hills."

"No, Jack, you're too tired and have to get up early. I'll be fine. And I really should stay. Zelda's also upset because her father called her today and told her he got married last night in Vegas."

"You're kidding?"

"No. The blushing bride is someone he hasn't known long. I think Zelda wanted to talk to me about it. And don't worry about where I am. This place was donated to a charity fundraiser. How bad can it be?"

"Bad."

Regan smiled. "You're right."

"Well, see if you can reach the assistant, then call me back."

"Okay." Regan hung up and went into the kitchen to see if any numbers were written on a pad somewhere. But there was nothing. It wasn't Zelda's house, so there were no notes on the refrigerator or counter, and nothing in the drawers. Norman's number was probably in Zelda's phone.

Regan went back upstairs, and crept into the bedroom. She'd left one small light on in the corner that wouldn't bother Zelda, but would let Regan keep an eye on her.

Zelda's head was moving from side to side on the pillow. "Oh," she groaned. "I'm so sick."

"Can I get you a little ginger ale?" Regan whispered. "It might help settle your stomach."

"No. I just wish the room would stop spinning."

"That's a horrible feeling," Regan commiserated. "You don't have any health problems I should know about, do you? Being sick like this makes you really dehydrated. Do you take any heart medicine or anything?"

"No. I never get sick." Zelda put her hands to her head. "It's so nice of you to stay. My mom thought you were so cute when you lost on the game show." Zelda tried to smile.

That does it, Regan thought. I'm not going anywhere.

It wouldn't have mattered if she'd tried to call Norman. He would never have heard his phone.

He'd made his way to a karaoke bar and was singing his heart out.

9

Regan was curled up in the chair next to Zelda's bed, her legs stretched out on a hassock. She'd made Zelda promise to wake her if she wanted to get up and go to the bathroom. Regan had placed a bucket next to the bed in case Zelda couldn't make the fifty yard dash.

But Regan couldn't fall asleep. She was worried about Zelda and the chair didn't exactly inspire slumber. The house was so quiet. I want to find out the history of this place, she thought. Being here is like going back in time. It feels like the set for an old Hollywood movie. Then her thoughts turned to Jack. He was so understanding. The second night we're in California I end up in sleeping in a chair in a mysterious house that probably has bodies buried in the backyard.

A loud crashing noise downstairs startled her into an upright position. She could feel her heart thumping in her chest.

Zelda was fast asleep.

There was no landline in the bedroom to call for help. There was a phone on the wall in the kitchen, but she wasn't even sure whether it worked. She grabbed her cell phone, which might or might not work downstairs. Regan walked over to the desk, grabbed a dull letter opener, and left the room. She stood in the hallway and listened.

Nothing. The whole house was again eerily quiet. Zelda had told Regan that the house didn't have an alarm system. Someone could have opened one of the windows on the ground floor and gotten in. I probably should have gone around and made sure every window and door was locked, but I didn't want to leave Zelda for long. Regan's mind was racing. I could call Jack, but then again, I can't call Jack unless I go downstairs. Maybe I can text him but he might not hear it. In any case, it would take him time to get here. I know he'd call the LAPD and have a patrol car race over, but I don't want to involve the police for no reason.

I've got to go check. Regan started down the stairs. She stopped at the bottom and waited. Whatever made that noise couldn't have been too far away from where I am right now, she reasoned, otherwise I wouldn't have heard it. To her left, the door to the bathroom was partially ajar. She gave it a slight push. Slowly it creaked open. Regan flipped on the light.

What a sight!

The shower curtain was in a heap in the tub, ornate heavy metal hooks scattered all around, the rusted rod now sticking out sideways. A decorative glass vase that Regan remembered seeing on the vanity had shattered on the floor.

Regan breathed a deep sigh of relief, laughed nervously, then shut the door. *This place is falling apart. That mess can wait until the morning.*

Emboldened, Regan went around the ground floor checking all the windows and doors. Luckily there was no basement. By the back door in the kitchen she noticed the bowl with her car keys. She'd seen them earlier, when she'd been looking for Norman's number. She'd been in such a hurry. *Surely the valet brought my car back up from the street. That's what they usually do at these kind of parties.* She peeked out the window but couldn't tell whether her car was there. It was too dark.

She opened the back door and stepped outside. The only sound was a light wind rustling the trees. Shocked, she realized that there was only one car in the driveway, Zelda's.

The valet didn't bring my car back? That's crazy. If they brought it back and someone stole it, that would be unbelievable. Why wouldn't they take Zelda's Mercedes? I know car thieves don't go as much for the luxury vehicles, but come on!

Should I go down the street and see if it's there? she asked herself. *If something happens to that rental, it's going to be a real pain.* Decisively, she went back to the kitchen, grabbed the keys, walked outside, and started down the path. When she reached the driveway, she slowed down. The outside lights were off and the pavement descended into darkness. Pitch darkness. There were no street lights.

I can't do this, she decided. Jack would be really upset it he knew I went wandering down a dark unfamiliar road at this time of night. If the car's not there in the morning, it's not there. It's just a car. She turned, went back in the house, and double locked the door.

Another troubling thought was swirling around her head. What made Zelda so sick? Something she ate? Regan went over to the pink refrigerator and opened it. All the leftovers were wrapped in plastic bags or aluminum foil. She shut the door. I know Zelda could have eaten something earlier today that she had a bad reaction to later, but her illness came on so fast.

Upstairs she was glad to see that Zelda was still asleep. Regan sat back on the chair, pulled the blanket over her, and tried to get comfortable.

Down the street, in the woods near her car, someone was anxiously waiting for Regan to leave the party. He was hoping she wasn't spending the night at the house. Why would she? She was staying in a luxury hotel in Beverly Hills.

With each passing minute he grew more agitated.

She should mind her own business, he thought. I'll teach her a lesson.

One way or the other, I'll get it done.

Friday, October 5th

10

When Regan opened her eyes, once again it took her a moment to realize where she was. The first clue was that she felt like a pretzel. Gray shadows giving the room a surreal atmosphere were the second. Oh yes, she thought. This ain't the Beverly Hills Island Hotel. Regan checked her watch. It was 7:10. Jack was probably on his way downtown to the meeting.

Regan dragged herself "out of chair," wishing it was out of bed. The sight of a sleeping Zelda reassured her that she wasn't in some sort of dream world. A few minutes later she located a bathroom downstairs that didn't have shattered glass all over the floor. Looking in the mirror, she sighed. I need to get back to the hotel after Zelda wakes up.

A new toothbrush that Zelda had given her the night before was in Regan's hand. After freshening up as much as she could, Regan grabbed her coat off the couch in the living room, and her keys from the kitchen. Let's hope the car is still there, she thought.

Outside, the air was brisk. Regan, in her heels, carefully made her way down the steep driveway. She turned and started up the block, enjoying the sound of the chirping birds. What a beautiful time of day, she thought. Everything is so peaceful.

Boyond the Scrumps estate, there were woods on either side of the street. Regan wondered why other houses hadn't been built. When she reached the top of the road, she spotted her car at the end of the block. All by itself.

"Yes!" she said aloud. "The day is starting out right." It felt good to walk and stretch her legs, after being cramped on that chair. When she reached the four-door sedan, and started to put the key in the door, a thought occurred to her. The valet last night had mentioned a hiking trail was right here. Should I take a quick look? If Jack and I decide to stay in LA for the weekend, a hike might be fun.

She walked around the car and started on a narrow path heading into the woods. Twigs crunched underneath her feet as her high heels started to sink into the soil. Maybe I shouldn't do this now, she thought. Turning around, a glint of silver caught her eye. It was a few feet off the walking path, and mostly covered by leaves. What's that? she wondered, slowly moving toward the shiny object. She leaned over, and carefully cleared away the leaves on top.

"Oh my God," Regan breathed.

She'd uncovered a long, shiny butcher knife.

What is that doing here? Regan wondered. It looks brand new. Once again, her heart started racing. Why would someone bring a knife like that into the woods? Did they hide it here? This is not good. Regan grabbed the handle, pointed the blade downward, and hurried back to the car. She opened the trunk, dropped the knife, and slammed the trunk shut. A minute later she was racing up Zelda's driveway.

It might be nothing, she reasoned, as she parked, got out, and went back into the kitchen. But that knife could be deadly. She double locked the door. If you go hiking, you might bring a pocket knife, but that's it. I'll talk to Jack later. The best thing to do would be to turn it over to the police. If the owner is looking for his butcher knife, let him go claim it at the precinct's lost and found.

Regan prepared a tray of tea and toast, enough for both her and Zelda. If she's not awake, I'll make more later. Regan headed upstairs and tiptoed into Zelda's room.

"Regan, hi." Zelda started to sit up.

"How do you feel?"

"A little wiped out."

"Tea?"

"Sounds great," Zelda said, propping herself up on the pillows. "I am thirsty." She sipped the tea Regan gave her and ate a slice of toast. "I'm glad I can get something down."

"I am, too," Regan agreed. Here goes, she thought. "Zelda, you mentioned yesterday we might go on a moonlight hike last night."

Zelda rolled her eyes. "Such big plans."

71

"You're not planning to go hiking in the next few days, are you?"

"Not the way I feel. But earlier this week I went for walks in the woods with my clients. Sometimes it's good to be out in nature and get all the cobwebs out of your head. This area is perfect for that. Even taking a walk on the block is great. No traffic!"

"Zelda, I just went down to the end of the road to get my car."

"One of the valets didn't bring it into the driveway last night?"

"No."

"That's terrible!"

"Well, maybe it's good they didn't. I walked down to take a look at the hiking trail but my sandals were getting stuck in the ground. I hadn't gone very far when I discovered a large butcher knife that was mostly hidden under some leaves."

"A large what?" Norman said excitedly as he strode into the room. "A knife? I was just coming up the steps and couldn't help but overhear."

"Oh, hello, Norman," Regan said. "Yes. I found a knife in the woods. And what's more troubling is that it obviously hasn't been there very long. It looked brand new."

Norman flopped in the chair.

Zelda glanced at him. "You look tired."

"It was very busy last night," Norman sniffed. "At least I'm not still in bed."

"Right after you left I got very sick," Zelda said reproachfully. "That's why Regan is here. She stayed with me."

"You got sick?"

"Yes."

"I'm so sorry," Norman said sincerely, as he put his hand to his mouth. "Regan, you should have called me. I would have come right back."

"It's okay," Regan said. "I wanted to stay."

"Tell us about the knife," Zelda urged.

"There's nothing much to say," Regan answered. "I put it in the trunk of my car. I just can't think of any good reason why it would be hidden under leaves in the woods. The valet said last night that people don't access the hiking trail from this street because they can't park here easily."

"Maybe we should hire a security guard," Norman said excitedly. "It's a good thing we're clearing out of here in a few days. What a waste of money this place is."

"It was for a good cause," Zelda protested. "Whatever it was."

Norman shrugged. "I don't remember. What do you think made you sick?"

"I don't know. I probably caught a bug."

Zelda's cell phone rang. She opened the drawer of her nightstand, grabbed it, and glanced at the caller ID.

"It's Rich," she said. "Hello . . . oh, thanks Rich,

73

it was fun, wasn't it? Yes, a lot of different people. You want to come by? Well, sure, I'll be here. Great. See you then." Zelda pressed disconnect and put down her phone. "Rich has some business he wants to discuss with me this afternoon."

"Shouldn't you rest?" Norman asked.

"He has something to talk to me about before he goes away for the weekend. Besides, if I just sit here I won't feel any better. I have to cancel my clients because it's not fair to charge for a session when I can't give them my best, but I can meet with Rich. Besides, we have to get ready for company that will be arriving late tonight."

Norman's eyes widened. "Company? Tonight? I'm exhausted."

"My father and his new wife."

"What?"

Zelda explained.

"Oh my God! He married her already!"

"Yes. They can use the bedroom downstairs at the end of the hall." Zelda shrugged. "It's too weird."

"While you're getting this place ready," Regan said, "you might want to take a look at the bathroom by the staircase. Last night the shower curtain collapsed into the tub."

"You took a shower there?" Norman asked quizzically. "You should have gone into one of the bedrooms and used a more private bathroom."

"I didn't shower. I was sitting here and heard a

crashing sound at three in the morning. The curtain rod is all rusted. It fell and knocked over a glass vase."

"Well, how perfect," Norman said, wrinkling his nose. "I'll take care of it. I guess."

Regan finished the last of her tea. "Speaking of showers, I think I'll head back to the hotel. But I do want you to be careful around here. Keep the doors locked."

"It's Friday," Norman said. "We'll be out of here Monday. Now that Zelda's father is coming, there will be a lot of people in the house."

"Regan," Zelda said disappointedly. "I feel terrible. You've been so good to me. Can you at least come back for lunch?"

"Zelda, shouldn't you just rest?"

"No, I'd much rather spend time with you. Besides, I wanted to talk to you about something."

"What?" Norman asked.

"Norman, I'm talking to Regan."

"Okay. Do you want me to leave?"

"No. You already know everything that goes on in my life." Zelda turned her head toward Regan. "I was wondering if I could hire you to find out a little about the woman my father married."

"Isn't it a little late?" Norman asked practically. "What good could it possibly do to have Regan start investigating now?"

Thanks, Norman, Regan thought.

"If there's something about her we should know,

it's not too late," Zelda said somewhat impatiently. "All I want to do is protect my father. If she checks out, she checks out. I hope they're happy!"

"All right, already," Norman said. "Take it easy."

Zelda looked at Regan. "What do you think?"

Poor Zelda, Regan thought. What a terrible position she's in. "I'd be happy to help you, but I do have plans for the weekend with Jack. Is it okay if I start the investigation next week?"

"Of course," Zelda said. "But come back for lunch."

11

Petunia, wrapped in a fluffy robe, was sipping coffee in her basement and admiring all the loot she'd received for her "charity fundraiser." After dinner last night Clarence had been so engrossed in the baseball game he barely noticed when she left the room. Petunia came straight downstairs to her office, turned on a large flat-screen television, and got to work. First she slit open the cardboard boxes containing the long folding tables she'd purchased at a discount store, threw the cardboard in a heap, and set up the tables against one wall. She placed all the donations on display and photographed each one.

With great care, she loaded the pictures from her camera to her computer, printed them out, and filed them in her desk. Every few minutes she grabbed the remote control and switched TV stations, hoping she'd find an infomercial for a get rich quick scheme or a phenomenal product that promised to change your life. It was easy for her to detect which ads were rip-offs. She was amazed at how quickly certain information flashed on and off the screen—information the consumer might be interested in, like the company's name.

In one corner of the room she'd already set up her Pet's Projects Studio consisting of a video camera on a tripod and a plain white backdrop. It was where she'd film promotions about her good works and post them on the Internet. She was learning how to change the background on the video screens so it appeared that she was in a much more exotic place than her basement. Petunia hoped to have many different identities as a do-gooder. Her notebook was full of ideas.

She yawned and took another sip of her triple mocha latte java, and smiled. I don't know why basements get a bad rap, she mused. Everyone scoffs about people who sit in their basements and post nasty anonymous comments on the Internet. That may be true, but basements are places where good things happen, too. Scientists carry out important experiments in basements. We store things in basements. People play Ping-Pong and shoot pool in basements. Some of us do our wash in basements. Bargain basements save us money, or at least they're supposed to.

And now, Petunia thought, putting down her coffee and stretching her arms, I'm going to launch a successful business of my own in my basement. I'm entering this game late in life but hopefully I'll figure out how to make up for lost time. How many companies, even if they're legitimate, started out small?

One step at a time, she thought, as she tried to touch her toes but couldn't. For a second she pondered purchasing exercise equipment but immediately nixed the idea as a waste of her hard-earned money. *If I get rich, I'll hire a trainer, even though I'll still hate to exercise.* She stood straight up, took a large gulp of coffee, and immediately felt better. *I've got to get dressed,* she thought, *but first I need to check my horoscope.*

She sat down at the computer, put on her reading glasses, and started tapping at the keys like an old pro. On her favorite astrological web site the forecast for her sign wasn't great. It warned of taking on new projects. Petunia frowned, then quickly searched several more sites looking for a prediction for the day that would make her happy. It was no different than biting into a half dozen fortune cookies before finding one that tells you you're better than everyone else.

Finally, she found what she was searching for. *You are ready for a big change.* She read aloud. *Don't stay stuck in the past. Go with the times. No one deserves it more than you.* Petunia whooped. "I do deserve it!" she said aloud. "I do!"

It is time for me to go with the times. I stayed stuck in the past and didn't pursue my dreams while my kids lived at home. If I don't act now, it may be too late. I'm glad I took that computer class last year.

Petunia was lost in her thoughts. *The world has changed so much since I was a kid. Back then, there were no computers or cell phones. Televisions had rabbit ears to get better reception* on a lousy six or seven stations! Wait a minute, she said to herself. What did all the hardcore scam artists do before the dawn of cable television and then the Internet? They must have been so unfulfilled! The Internet really opened the floodgates for people who wanted to get their hands on other people's money. Now they could reach into the pocket of someone on the other side of Mother Earth in no time flat!

The door at the top of the basement steps opened. "Petunia!" Clarence bellowed.

"Here!"

"Jade is on the phone."

Petunia deliberately didn't have a phone in the basement. She didn't want anyone other than herself or Clarence to have a reason to go down there. When her kids came home for a visit, she planned to put the cameras away and make the space appear to be a comfy office where Mom liked to occasionally dabble on the computer. "Jade's on the phone?"

"That's what I said."

"I'm coming."

Jade, their youngest, had graduated from a college in San Diego five months earlier. To Petunia's dismay, she wanted to commute to school, thus putting off her parents' plans to move north for four years. Now Jade was in a tiny country Petunia had never heard of, thousands of miles away, teaching English to needy children. I don't know where she came from, Petunia often thought.

At the top of the steps Clarence handed her the phone, then kissed her on the cheek. "See you later. You'd better hurry. You'll be late for work." "I know," Petunia said, giving him a playful push. She held the phone to her ear. "Jade, honey, how's it going? You're loving it still. It's only been a couple of weeks you've been there. The kids are so cute? Oh, great, I'm so proud of you . . . right . . . right . . . your sister is fine. She's like you, saving the world, just closer to home." Petunia laughed. "Honey, I was wondering. Why don't you take a picture of your class and send it to me? I'd love to see their little faces. Take lots of photos, okay?" Petunia laughed. "Of course I want you to be in one or two of the pictures!"

No more than that, Petunia thought. Or I'll edit you out.

12

Back at the hotel, Regan took the elevator to the sixth floor, then headed down a long hallway. A maid's cart was parked suspiciously close to her room. Oh, please, Regan thought, don't let her be in there now. I'm dying to take a shower.

With a sigh of relief, Regan passed the cart full of fresh towels and toiletry samples, taking a quick glance into the room next to hers where the maid was cleaning. She was about to fire up the vacuum. Quickening her pace, Regan let herself into her room. It hadn't been cleaned yet. Just in time, Regan thought. The maid can come back after I leave.

She put her purse on the desk and took off her shoes. Looking at the unmade bed she could tell that Jack had barely moved from his side. Oh, Regan thought wistfully. He must have been so tired. It feels strange to think he's come and gone. She shrugged. We have all weekend to be together.

They had texted each other earlier, and decided to stay in Los Angeles tonight. The plan was to have dinner in Beverly Hills at an Italian restaurant, then tomorrow morning they'd figure out what they wanted to do. I'm so glad we won't be scrambling to check out this evening, Regan thought. We've hardly spent any time enjoying this beautiful hotel.

She pressed the DO NOT DISTURB button, ordered breakfast from room service, then headed into the shower. The sprays of hot water coming from all directions felt great, especially on her achy neck and shoulders. She could have stood there all day. After several minutes she turned off the faucets and grabbed a towel. She dried off and wrapped herself in one of the hotel's terrycloth robes. Now I notice how hungry I am! That slice of toast at Zelda's didn't cut it.

Regan decided to rest until room service arrived. She lay down on the side of the bed where Jack had slept, then turned her head so her cheek was resting on his pillow, breathing in his scent. I wish he were here.

Her thoughts turned to Zelda. What she's going through would be a lot easier if she had someone like Jack. Zelda has nice friends, and Norman certainly provides interesting companionship, but she has no one to really lean on. She's pretty much on her own. To think just yesterday she found out that her father married someone he hasn't known very long. Zelda was upset that he hadn't talked to her first. I can't imagine being in that position. Regan shuddered. It would never happen, she told herself. Then she laughed out loud. The thought of her father getting married in a drive-through chapel in Las Vegas was so absurd, it was funny. No, if my father ended up alone, it would be sad for both of us. I'd have to expect the unexpected, but certainly not that.

Regan pulled the sheets under her chin. I'll help Zelda as much as I can. I certainly hope that financial adviser is doing well by her. He wasn't slick, but that doesn't mean he's honest. Maybe I should ask Zelda a few questions about her business affairs when I see her today. She's worried enough about her father to have his new wife checked out, but I wonder what she knows about the people working for her. I'm also interested to hear about her coaching.

Suddenly Regan sat up. I hope the hotel staff doesn't do a security check and open the trunk of the car! When the attendant drove off with it, the knife completely slipped my mind. I should have just dropped it off at the police station. I'll do that on the way back to Zelda's. I don't have to wait for Jack. By the time he gets back here we'll want to start our weekend. Besides, I've been in the police stations around here before. I did work in this town.

Feeling restless, Regan brought her laptop over to the bed. She leaned against the headboard and started to research the Scrumps estate. Nothing came up. Is it owned by a trust? she wondered. If they're not using it, why don't they sell it? They have that whole block to themselves. There's so much privacy. Maybe too much! The lingering question in the back of her mind surfaced again. What was someone doing in those woods with a knife like that?

Her cell phone rang. It was her mother, Nora.

"Hi, Mom."

"Regan, hi. Just thought I'd see how your trip was going so far."

"Well, it's been a little unusual."

"Oh? I'm all ears."

"Remember when I was on that game show?" Regan began.

"Of course I do. You missed out on the big money. Your consolation prizes, which provided you little consolation, were electric curlers you never used, and a dozen boxes of macaroni noodles."

"You have the memory of an elephant."

"It helps with my writing. So what about the game show?"

"Someone I got friendly with those few days at the studio, her name is Zelda. . . ."

"Wait, wasn't she on after you?"

"Yes."

"I remember. Don't forget, we've played that tape more than once over the years."

"I know you love to embarrass me," Regan said, her tone amused.

"No, I don't. The expression on your face when you lost was priceless. You looked like you wanted to strangle the woman who gave you that bad clue."

"I did want to strangle her. Anyway, I ran into Zelda yesterday."

Nora listened as Regan recounted the tale, interrupting only occasionally. "Eight million dollars? Not bad."

"Can you believe it?" Regan asked without waiting for an answer. She finished the story, leaving out the juicy bit about discovering a butcher knife in the woods.

"Her father got married in the back of a taxi at a drive-through wedding chapel?" Nora blurted. Clearly she found this to be the most astonishing piece of news.

"Yes!"

"Wow. My word." Nora paused, then asked quietly, "Regan, can you just picture your father?"

"I thought the same thing! Can you see Daddy, with a flower in the lapel of one of his black suits, sitting in the back of a beat-up cab, waiting on line at the drive-up window?"

"Not with the meter running."

Regan lowered her voice. "I'll have fries with that."

They both started to laugh. Their beloved Luke was so dignified.

"I'm sorry," Nora finally said, trying to contain her laughter. "I'm not making fun of Zelda's troubles. And the only way your father would ever end up in that situation would be over my dead body, so I'm laughing at myself, too."

"I know, Mom. Zelda was actually trying to joke about it herself, quoting lines from songs about how love can make you do crazy things. But it's not as funny for her because she's not imagining it."

"The poor dear," Nora replied. "Regan, I don't envy you. I sincerely hope you find nothing scandalous about this woman and Zelda learns to like her. But if that's not the case, I hope whatever you find is bad enough that Zelda's father will want to get out fast. Anything in between could be very sticky."

"I have the feeling Zelda wants me to find something truly awful."

"Well, do you think you'll head up to wine country tomorrow?" Nora asked, changing the subject.

"I'm not sure."

"It's funny. The other day I signed several books for fundraisers. You know me with my map on the wall. I love to see where the books are going. One of the requests was from a town north of Los Angeles. The letter struck me as being a little odd, but I sent the book anyway. I figured I may as well since my new assistant had already addressed the envelope."

"Why did it seem odd?"

"It just. . . ."

There was a loud knock at Regan's door. "Room service!"

Regan put her hand over the phone. "Coming," she called. "Mom, I have to go. My breakfast is here."

Three more knocks, even louder. "ROOM SERVICE!"

"COMING!" Regan yelled.

"Regan, let me know what happens."

"I will."

When Regan pulled open the door, a waiter was smiling from ear to ear, a sense of peace and calm emanating from his being. "Good morning, Mrs. Reilly. Are you having a good day so far?"

"Couldn't be better."

"May I come in with your breakfast?"

No, I'll eat it in the hallway, Regan wanted to answer. Instead, she smiled back at him. "Of course, please come in. I'll hold the door."

Two seconds later, her cell phone began to ring.

The waiter slowly pushed the breakfast table forward, but the wheels got stuck on the threshold. "Oops," he said, as the glass and silverware jiggled. "Let's try again." He slowly backed up the table, then shoved it forward.

"Got it?" Regan asked, then ran for her phone. Before she reached it, the ringing stopped. She checked the number—Jack had called! She dialed right back but it went to voice mail. He hadn't left a message. He probably made a quick call when he had a minute, then shut off his phone. She wanted so much to talk to him.

"Mrs. Reilly, may I pour you a cup of coffee?"

"No!" Regan wanted to tell him, trying to calm her frustration. Then she almost laughed. *I bet I have the same batty expression on my face as when I lost on that game show. There's no doubt about it—love and money can make you crazy.*

13

After Regan left, Zelda left messages for her clients, then fell asleep again. An hour later she was up, heading to the bathroom, feeling very dizzy. I'll have to go right back to bed, she thought. Norman wasn't surprised to find her there when he returned to the room.

"I can't stand up for long."

"I told you," he said, not unkindly. "You're not going to be back on your feet until tomorrow."

Zelda's arms were crossed, covering her eyes. "What could have caused this?"

"I don't think food poisoning strikes right away, so it probably wasn't anything you ate at the party. But if we start getting phone calls from sick party guests, you'd better check your insurance policy. What did you eat yesterday?"

"Nothing for breakfast. When I was out shopping, I had a cheesesteak sandwich. Last night I was so busy I only had a couple hors d'oeuvres and a small piece of ham."

"Don't you advocate the importance of a healthy diet to your clients?"

"At times, I stray."

"Do you want me to cancel lunch with Regan?"

"No! I have to talk to her about Bobby Jo.

Regan won't mind having a sandwich up here. I certainly won't feel like eating."

"What about Rich?"

"He's only stopping by for a little while. He can come up here and speak to me."

"I'll run to the store and pick up sandwich makings and a salad. I don't think we should offer Regan leftovers. Especially if they cause food poisoning. I'd better throw everything out."

Zelda nodded. "Get me some of the chicken noodle soup we love. Hopefully I'll be able to have that later."

"Okay. Don't worry, Zelda, you'll feel better soon."

"I hope so. Norman, do you think someone could have spiked my drink?"

"Why would anyone do that?"

"I don't know."

"Your friends wouldn't do that. The help wouldn't have any reason to do it. Rich and Heather and Gladys certainly want you to stay healthy, that's for sure. If you die, they won't be handling your money." He chuckled. "Bobby Jo will."

"Norman, why are you tormenting me?"

"I'm sorry. I shouldn't have said that. It was a stupid joke."

"If you must know, you're in my will, but that could change because I plan to amend it."

"What? Zelda, you're my friend. I didn't mean to—"

91

"Listen, would you?" Zelda interrupted.

"Okay."

"I left generous gifts to you and a couple of other close friends. Everything else goes to my father. But I don't want that woman to get her hands on it. I don't know everything about trusts but I know enough to know that I'd like to set one up for my father. If I die he can take money from the trust until he dies. Then it will revert back to my estate and go to you and my other friends. You should be grateful to Bobby Jo. If she hadn't come along I wouldn't be making these changes. Most of my money would go straight to my father. It would never end up back with you."

Norman had been pointing in the air with his index finger, making an imaginary trail of the money. "Zelda," he stammered, "I'd be desolate if something happened to you! All jokes aside, I'd rather have you in my life than your money in my bank account. I mean it!"

"I know that, Norman. I really do. That's why I trust you, and I only want the best for you. You haven't seemed happy lately."

Norman flopped in the chair. "It's hard not knowing which way my life is going. I love working for you, but it's not a career and I need more."

"What would you really like to do?"

Norman looked at the ground. He tapped his fingers against the chair. "I don't know."

"Yes, you do. It's the question I ask everyone I coach. What would you really like to do?"

"Sing," Norman said in a tiny voice.

"I can't hear you."

"Sing," Norman said a little bit louder.

"What did you say?"

"SING," Norman shouted.

"There you go! You want to sing?"

"YES! I feel alive when I sing! There's nothing like hearing the applause."

"Applause? When do you hear applause?"

"Late at night in karaoke bars."

"It's a start."

"It is! And I'm taking singing lessons, but I can barely afford them."

"What do I always tell my students?"

"Go for your dream."

"That's right."

"But sometimes going for your dream is a little tough on the pocketbook."

"I'll pay for your lessons."

"You will?"

"Yes. If you must know, I don't charge some of my students. And I help them with certain expenses."

"You do?"

"Yes. Only the ones who really need it. I won't do it forever. They all say they'll pay me back. We'll see."

"You're always working so hard with your coaching. It's not as if you need the money."

"I enjoy it. Like you with your singing. It makes me feel good to help people build their confidence. Then all they need is a little push."

"And a little dough."

"Norman!"

"Sorry."

"At least I don't have to worry about you being nice to me for my money."

"That's for sure."

Zelda laughed. "I've always felt that you've been glad for me about the money. Not many people are. It's human nature. There's a lot of jealousy."

"I never begrudged you a nickel. And . . . and . . . and . . . I've stayed out of your financial matters."

"That's true, you have. You know what, Norman?"

"What?"

"Sometimes having this much money is more trouble than it's worth."

"I'd like a shot at it."

"I'm serious. Take, for example, the fundraiser I went to that had the auction for this house. I didn't know anyone there. I don't even know how they got my address or phone number."

"You get on a list. Then you're toast."

"I always buy tickets to these events. And then I feel guilty if I don't spend more money when I'm there. That's why we're sitting in this house now."

"It's an experience."

"That it is. Listen, why don't you run into town and get the shopping done? I'd also like you to stop at my apartment. Whatever information I have about the charity, and the paperwork for this house, is on the desk in my office. I'd like Regan to take a look at it."

"Good idea. This place is a dump."

"It's not that bad. I think I'll try and get some sleep now."

"Okay. I love you, Zelda."

"I love you too, Norman." She smiled. "If you ever keep anything from me like my father did, I'll kill you."

Norman howled as he left the room.

14

The morning after Maggie worked at the Scrumps estate, she slept until 9:00. Her studio apartment was in a nice-enough complex on Kings Road in West Hollywood, but her unit was below ground. As a result, it was often difficult to discern what the weather was like, or even the time of day. Sliding glass doors ran the length of the small room, and opened onto a narrow patio that faced a cement wall. At the top of the wall security bars were welded to the building. The only natural light that reached Maggie's apartment passed through those bars.

Coffee, Maggie thought, I need coffee. She pulled on a pair of sweats, grabbed her keys, and slipped a ten dollar bill in her pocket as she left the apartment. She double locked both cylinders, then sauntered down the hall to a metal door that led outside. She pushed it open, ascended a small staircase, and stepped onto the sidewalk.

"The world is still here," she mumbled as she breathed in fresh air and started up the block. It's hard to tell what's going on when I'm down in that cell. She had made the space as homey as she could, but it still felt so confining. Maggie liked to get up and out first thing in the morning and pick up a cup of coffee. It was an expense, but a necessary one. She did it for her sanity. Besides, Gelson's Market was only a block away and their coffee was the best. Today I might even treat myself to a banana muffin, Maggie mused. One of the best things about being a character actress was not having to agonize over every morsel of food you put in your mouth.

On the street she passed several people out walking their dogs. Most of them nodded and smiled. My apartment might not be the greatest, but I love this neighborhood.

She could have gotten a better apartment if she was willing to live with a roommate, but one bad experience had put her off that forever. Before she left a suburb of Chicago for Los Angeles, she'd found an apartment online. A middle-aged woman who lived in a modern two-bedroom on Wilshire Boulevard in Westwood wanted a roommate to help cover expenses. She turned out to be a weirdo who stayed up all night with the television blaring while she drank pitchers of margaritas. Within a week she stormed into Maggie's room at 2:00 A.M., waving a pair of scissors and accusing Maggie of stealing her organic limes.

Maggie was terrified. She would never close her eyes in that apartment again. When the woman retreated, Maggie locked her door, packed her bags, and waited. The wacko finally went out "to meet a client" at noon. At 12:01 Maggie hightailed it out of there. She never looked back. She never looked for another roommate, either.

Inside Gelson's, Maggie headed straight to the bakery section. The fresh breads and pastries smelled great. *I may as well indulge*, she decided, ordering a muffin with her coffee. *I worked hard last night.*

Walking back down the block, she thought about the previous evening. That older woman Gladys was a hoot. She came into the kitchen three different times to say hello and see if any of her favorite hors d'oeuvres were left. When she found out the help were all aspiring actors, she told them she had wanted to be an actress but her parents wouldn't let her. Instead, they sent her to secretarial school to learn bookkeeping.

"I never should have listened," she said as she popped a scallop wrapped with bacon into her mouth.

"I read an article about several older women who went into acting later in life and really did well," Maggie had told her. "It's never too late. Especially if you're funny."

The two of them exchanged numbers.

Back in the abyss, one of several nicknames Maggie had given her apartment, she sat at her computer, took the lid off her coffee, and started perusing the latest audition notices. Like most young actors, she was doing as much as she could to find work on her own. She had an agent who couldn't get her arrested, which was especially irksome considering her living conditions. Maggie didn't have her Screen Actors Guild card which made things even more difficult. She couldn't get a union job because she wasn't in SAG, but she couldn't get into SAG until she had a union job.

Non-union projects were good for gaining experience and building a reel. But because those projects weren't subject to strict rules and regulations, you never knew what you were getting into.

Maggie sipped her coffee and scrolled down the page. Why wasn't I born gorgeous? she wondered as she took a bite of her muffin. Well, I know I can do comedy. She jotted down the contact information on several roles she thought she'd be right for. Nothing that's going to win me an Academy Award, she thought, but work is work. It's also about making connections for future jobs.

After Maggie forwarded her picture and resume to all the projects she was interested in, she went back to look at the roles for older women that she had noticed on a couple of non-union projects. There were two different parts that had Gladys's name written all over them. Maggie got up and retrieved her phone from the table next to the bed. I'll call her right now! Gladys should send in her picture. Give acting a whirl. There shouldn't be too much competition. Someone Gladys's age who was non-union was either just starting out or no Sarah Bernhardt.

But as Maggie started to make the call, she hesitated, wondering if she was being too pushy. The conversation about Gladys wanting to be an actress could have just been party talk. Gladys has a job and would probably be too embarrassed to send in her photo, even if she's interested. I know what I'll do, Maggie thought. This might turn out great!

At the party the night before, when Norman was in the living room balancing his dinner plate on his lap, the four workers had taken pictures of each other in front of those crazy hot pink appliances. They'd all prepared food in state of the art kitchens in mansions around Los Angeles, and in some homes that were decidedly less grand, but none of them had seen anything like the kitchen at the Scrumps estate. They'd also taken pictures of the cracked linoleum floor. The third time Gladys came wandering through, she caught them in the act.

"Isn't this place something?" she'd laughed, and offered to take a group shot. Then Maggie asked Gladys if she'd be in a picture with her.

"You don't want a picture of me," Gladys said.

"Yes, I do. Come on. Fast. We don't have much time. Norman will be back any second."

The other waitress snapped several photos.

Gladys turned out to be quite photogenic and a bit of a ham.

I'll use one of those pictures, Maggie thought. I'll cut myself out, enlarge the image of Gladys, and sent it out with my contact number. If she gets an audition, I'll call her with the good news.

Boy, will she be surprised!

15

Regan walked into the police precinct closest to the Scrumps estate. An officer with dark hair and a mustache sitting at the front desk looked up at her. "Can I help you?"

"I'm sure you can," Regan said, showing him her ID. "I'm a private investigator. My name is Regan Reilly. I used to have an office in Hollywood but now I live in New York City. My husband is head of the Major Case Squad there. We're in town because he has meetings with the police commissioner."

The officer raised his eyebrows. "Really?" He seemed friendly but guarded.

"Yes," Regan continued, "a friend of mine was at a fundraiser and bid on and won a week's stay at a home up in the Hills. It's called the Scrumps estate. I was there last night for a party she gave and stayed overnight because she got sick. Early this morning I went out to move my car, which was parked at the end of her block. There are no other houses. It's fairly isolated."

"What's the address?"

Regan told him. "Before I got into my car I wanted to take a look at a hiking trail someone told me about last night. I started into the woods, then decided against it. A flash of silver under a pile of leaves caught my eye. I didn't expect it to be a large butcher knife that looks brand new."

The officer groaned. "Wonderful. Where is the knife right now?"

"In my trunk. I didn't think it was wise to walk into a police station brandishing a knife like that. And I didn't want to be carrying a concealed weapon." Regan smiled.

"You've got that right. It's obviously a concern that someone would bring a weapon like that into those woods. There are a lot of people who go hiking alone."

"That's what I thought."

Regan was introduced to Detective Hector Ramone, who wrote up the report and then accompanied her to her car. When Regan popped the trunk, he whistled, then pulled on a latex glove. "This knife isn't for carving your girl-friend's initials into a tree," he observed wryly. With care he lifted the knife out of the trunk and placed it in a plastic bag. "I'm sure they'll step up patrols in the area. You say your friend will be at that house until Monday?"

"Yes."

"She's not alone, is she?"

"No. Her assistant is staying with her. Do you know anything about the Scrumps estate?"

"Not much. To my knowledge no one has ever called us from there with any problems."

"It seems like the house hasn't been lived in for

years, and it's not in the best condition. I think it's strange that someone would donate a stay there for charity. The Ritz it's not."

He laughed. "I'll see what I can find out."

Regan gave him her card. "If you come across anything interesting, please let me know."

"I will."

When Regan pulled out of the precinct parking lot, the sense of threat surrounding the knife seemed alarmingly real.

16

After Norman left, Rich telephoned Zelda. "It turns out I had to meet a client nearby. Do you mind if I come over now?"

"No, but I have to warn you, my stomach's acting up. I'm still in bed."

"That's fine."

"But wait a minute," Zelda said. "Norman's about to leave for the store. My friend Regan who you met last night is coming over for lunch and we need food. I don't think I can make it downstairs to let you in."

"Can he wait a few minutes until I get there?"

"I suppose." When she hung up, Zelda called Norman's cell phone. He was in the kitchen heading out the door. "Rich is on his way. Stick around a few minutes and let him in."

"I'll leave the door unlocked and wait in my car." Norman was dying to put a CD in his car stereo and belt out a tune. With Zelda paying for my singing lessons, he thought, the sky's the limit.

"That's fine. You know what, you don't have to wait."

"Yes, I do!"

"Okay. I'll see you later."

Norman was snapping his fingers and singing along with the Jersey Boys when Rich pulled up the driveway in his snooty sports car and parked next to him. Norman rolled down his passenger window. "The door's unlocked. Lock it behind you," he called out.

"I will," Rich said with a wave as he reached for his briefcase. He watched as Norman disappeared down the driveway, walked inside, and went upstairs.

"Zelda?" he called as he knocked on her open door.

"Come on in."

"I'm so sorry you're not feeling well."

"Something didn't agree with me."

"I stopped at a health food store and bought you some tea," he said, taking a paper cup out of a brown bag. "They say it's great for an upset stomach."

Zelda sat up and took a sip. "It's different," she said, then took another sip. "I don't mean to be rude, Rich, but as they say, it's not my cup of tea. I like the basic brands. Nothing too exotic."

Rich laughed. "No problem. I was hoping it would make you feel better."

"I appreciate it, I really do." Zelda's head was back on the pillow. "Leave it there. Maybe I'll try another sip."

"Sure," Rich said. "It won't hurt my feelings if you don't drink it."

Zelda sat up. She tried the tea again, then shook her head. "Sorry, Rich."

"That's fine." He put the lid back on the cup, then placed the cup back into the bag. "You win some, you lose some," he joked. "I can see that you really don't feel well, so I won't take much of your time. Heather and I are heading out of town this afternoon and won't be back until the middle of next week. I wanted to talk to you about a few things first."

"I want to talk to you, too. I need to change my will."

"Does that have something to do with your father getting married?" he asked solicitously.

"It has everything to do with my father getting married." Tears stung Zelda's eyes.

Rich sat in the chair next to the bed. "I'm so sorry about that, Zelda," he said gently. "As you know, my mother died when I was young. My father remarried a couple years later. What I never told you was that at the beginning I couldn't stand his new wife."

"Really?"

"Yes. I never talk about it because she turned out to be wonderful. Maybe your father's wife will become a good friend of yours."

"I doubt it. But she'll get her big chance to win me over soon. They're coming here tonight."

"They are?" he asked. "Already?"

"Yes. They wanted to get a look at this crazy house."

Rich laughed. "This place is interesting, that's

for sure. But, tell me, what do you want to do with your will?"

Zelda explained her idea about the trust.

"Makes sense. Heather's law firm handles trusts. She knows the ins and outs better than I do. I'll talk to her about it this weekend."

"Are you two getting serious?"

"I think so. Heather is special."

"Everyone around me is tying the knot. If you plan to get married, could you please let me know in advance?"

"You'll be the first to know. And I can't wait to dance at your wedding."

"Oh, please. So why did you want to see me today?" Zelda asked wearily. All she wanted to do was escape the world and sleep.

"Well, I was going over your accounts. You've been so generous to charities and your students."

"I believe in giving back."

"Which is honorable. But we have to look to your future. You've said you want to be conservative, but there is no growth in keeping too much of your money in cash or treasuries. If your money doesn't grow, then your account just goes down, down, down all the time. It might seem like you have a lot of money, but you're still young. It won't last forever if you don't. . . ."

Zelda's eyes drooped while Rich blathered on about the economy. She didn't understand most of what he was saying.

"I think it would be wise for you to invest in new companies. They carry a greater degree of risk, but if successful would yield a great return. Who ever thought that a company like Google would make so many people rich? People who invested in Google early on must be patting themselves on the back. I just got word of a company that is bringing out a brand new vitamin. It is going to take over the market because it's a vitamin aimed at everyone, not a vitamin just for kids, or women, or men. And it's the only vitamin anyone will ever need. The scientist who developed this miracle pill said the human body needs certain nutrients no matter the age or gender. This is going to blow all the other brands out of the water. If you're interested you've got to get in on it today."

"You think I should invest in vitamins?" Zelda asked when he finally stopped talking. She could barely keep her eyes open.

"I'd be lying if I said no. Zelda, I want you to build your wealth, not deplete it. Nothing ventured, nothing gained."

Zelda signed a piece of paper she didn't read. Her glasses were in the drawer and she was too tired to get them out. All she wanted to do was sleep. While Rich stuck the paper in his briefcase, she started to drift off. I should stay awake until he leaves, she told herself.

But when she opened her eyes he was gone.

17

While Bobby Jo was in the bathroom getting ready to go down to the breakfast buffet, Roger waited in the living room of their suite. The manager of the hotel had upgraded them on their return from the drive-through chapel.

"What happy news!" he'd said as Bobby Jo announced to the front desk she'd be checking out of her room and into her husband's. "If you're giving up one of your rooms, then I really think you should be in one of our bridal suites, don't you?"

"Yippee," Bobby Jo had exulted.

My head is killing me, Roger thought, the sight of an empty bottle of champagne in an ice bucket on the coffee table making him queasy. The last two days we've done so much drinking. I don't think I'll ever want another sip of the bubbly. He was also starting to feel a little funny inside, and it wasn't just the hangover. Three months of nonstop Bobby Jo, then the quickie wedding. He felt like everything was a blur. This morning he missed his first wife more than ever.

"Honey, I'll be just another minute or two," Bobby Jo called.

"Take your time," he answered quickly, feeling ashamed. Bobby Jo's a good woman. Her husband died years ago and she's still got a smile on her face. It's not fair for me to be thinking about Zelda's mother. Nothing is going to bring her back. I've got to live in the present, although maybe I should have taken this more slowly. And I know leaving Zelda out wasn't right. The two of us went through a lot together. I would hate it if she called me and said she'd gotten married. Heck, I want to be the proud father and walk her up the aisle.

Roger unfolded the newspaper and thumbed through it. His eyes focused on an article about divorce. "Second marriages are more likely to fail than first marriages," it began. Roger threw down the paper. Marriage is a commitment. You have to work at it.

The bathroom door flew open. *"Ready!"* Bobby Jo enthused. "Do you think these shorts make me look fat?"

Roger laughed. "Not at all. You look beautiful."

Bobby Jo came over and kissed him. "Let's go. I'm starving."

The restaurant was large and ornate, with bright orange walls and crystal chandeliers. Buzzing, beeping, and musical sounds emanated from the casino. "Hello to the newlyweds," the maître d' greeted them, flashing a smile.

"We've been married thirty-six hours," Bobby Jo crowed.

"That's beautiful. Follow me."

He led them to a private table, in the corner. "Now," he said as they were seated. "Can I get you each a mimosa? Or perhaps a bottle of champagne?"

"Sure," Bobby Jo said excitedly. "Roger, should we get the bottle?"

Roger put up his hand. "I think I'd better hold off. No champagne for me."

Bobby Jo ordered a mimosa.

"A mimosa it is."

"And I'll have coffee," Roger said.

"Perfect. I'll put in the order. Enjoy."

"Come on, Roger. I'm starving." Bobby Jo led the way to the buffet table.

There was every kind of breakfast food imaginable. Roger ordered a vegetable omelet. While he was waiting, he made toast for himself. Bobby Jo stacked her plate with blueberry pancakes, then picked at the pan of bacon, choosing the crispiest pieces she could find. Returning to the table, they dug into their food.

"I can't wait to see the house Zelda is staying in," Bobby Jo finally said after polishing off half her plate. "I'd really love to leave here right after breakfast."

"Honey, remember we talked about how dangerous it is to drive through the desert at the hottest time of day?"

"You're right. What time should we leave, then?"

"Around four."

"Sounds good. We should be there by nine. Maybe we can go to a late dinner. Los Angeles has so many great restaurants with lots of action."

"Let's see what time we get there and then decide."

Bobby Jo sipped her coffee. "I have so much to do when we get back. First, I have to get rid of my apartment. All my things won't fit in your place. Maybe we should buy a new house."

Roger cleared his throat. "Bobby Jo, I don't think that's a good idea at our age."

She smiled. "Don't forget. I'm six years younger."

"Yes, you are. Well, at my age, I don't want to take on any debt."

"I'm sure Zelda would lend you the money."

"I'm sure Zelda would do anything I wanted. But I don't want to borrow from her. If we ever needed money, she'd be right there. But a bigger house is something I'm not interested in."

"You're right," Bobby Jo agreed. "What was I thinking?"

"We'll have a nice life. I'd love to travel again."

"Me too! I didn't mean to look greedy." Bobby Jo rubbed his hand with her finger. "You're so neat and I have so much stuff. That's all I was thinking. But don't worry, I'll get rid of as much as I can." She rolled her eyes. "It's not going to be easy."

"Don't worry, honey. I'll make room for you."

Bobby Jo pushed back her chair. "I'm going up to get some fruit. Would you like anything?"

"No."

Roger watched her walk over to the buffet table. A busboy with a tray of dirty dishes almost ran into her. A plate fell to the floor. Bobby Jo leaned down and picked it up for him. She's a good woman. You made the right choice, Roger, he said to himself, you're getting the jitters for no reason. He turned back to the table. A few minutes later he picked up his phone and dialed Zelda. It rang and rang. Finally her voice mail answered.

"Hey, honey, it's Dad. Bobby Jo and I will be leaving Vegas around four. Just wanted to make sure everything was okay at your end. We thought we might take you out to dinner when we get there. Give me a call. I love you, sweetheart. Bye."

Bobby Jo returned to the table as he put down his phone. "You called Zelda?"

"Yes. Just to check in. My wife always liked to speak to Zelda every day."

Without a word Bobby Jo grabbed her napkin and placed it on her lap. She then folded her hands and looked over at Roger.

He waited.

"Roger," she said, her expression one he'd never seen before. "I'm your wife now. Till death do us part."

18

When Regan got out of her car at Zelda's, Norman was pulling up the driveway.

"Regan!" he yelled. "I hope I didn't keep you waiting!"

"Isn't Zelda inside?"

"She can't get out of bed. Whatever made her sick last night knocked the stuffing out of her."

"That's terrible. I hope she feels better soon," Regan replied. Her purse dangled over her shoulder, a carrying case that contained her laptop, portable printer, and iPad in her right hand. She grabbed one of the grocery bags from Norman's trunk with her free hand and followed him into the kitchen. A clock over the sink that matched the color of the appliances indicated the time was 12:05. "I'll see how Zelda is."

"Let me know when you'd like to have lunch."

"I will, thanks. I'm fine for now."

Upstairs all was quiet. Regan was surprised to find Zelda in a heavy sleep. She put down her carrying case, then pulled a piece of paper out of her purse and wrote a note.

Zelda, I'll be downstairs. Call me on my cell phone when you wake up. I hope it rings! I'll

check back in on you in a little while. Regan.
It's just after noon.

Norman was standing in front of the refrigerator, throwing the leftovers from the party into a trash bag.

"Zelda's in a dead sleep," Regan told him.

"She is?" Norman asked as he sniffed a package wrapped in aluminum foil, then dropped it into the garbage. "Her financial adviser came by when I was leaving. He probably bored her to death."

Regan laughed. "What do you mean?"

"When he gets started talking about stocks and bonds and blah blah blah blah blah, you'd better run for cover."

"That's his world," Regan noted, taking a better look around the kitchen. "I keep telling myself I should learn more about finance."

"You and me both. I've never ever balanced my checkbook." He peeked into another mound of food surrounded by tinfoil, then sniffed it. "I don't know why I'm bothering to check the leftovers from last night, since I'm throwing everything out anyway."

The package landed in the trash with a thud.

"You think Zelda got sick from something she ate?"

Norman shrugged. "Who knows? This morning Zelda asked me if she thought someone might have spiked her drink."

"She did?" Regan asked.

"Yes."

"But it was her party. That's the kind of thing that happens when you're out at bars or with people you just met. Do you think she's concerned about someone who was here?"

Norman pulled his head out of the refrigerator and looked straight into Regan's eyes. "You're right! She must be suspicious of somebody to even ask that question. I hope it's not me!"

"It's not you, Norman. She wouldn't have talked about having me check out her father's new wife in front of you if she didn't trust you."

"Are you sure?"

"Every instinct I have tells me that she trusts you implicitly." Regan smiled. "Whether she should or not is another story."

"Regan!"

"I'm just kidding. Tell me about the financial adviser who was here today."

"His name is Rich Willowwood. You met him last night."

"Where does he work?"

"He has his own investment company in the valley."

"Where did she meet him?"

"He advised the woman who left Zelda her money. Tell me you're not going to love the person who forwards you a check for eight million."

Regan thought for a moment. "He doesn't even look like he's thirty years old yet. He couldn't have been handling her money for long."

"I guess not."

"How old was that woman?"

Norman rolled his eyes. "This is an exasperating topic for me. I should have been nicer to her."

"How old?"

"She was ninety-two. But she didn't look it. Boy, was she feisty."

"What was her name?"

"Florence Natalie."

"Do you have any idea who was handling Natalie's money before Rich?"

"Who was handling Natalie's money before Rich was born?" Norman asked, pushing his glasses back on his nose.

Regan shrugged. "I guess all that matters is whether he's doing a good job."

"I never got involved in Zelda finances," Norman pronounced. "I don't want to seem like I'm looking for anything from her. She knows that."

"I'm sure she does. When she wakes up I'll ask her more about Rich. What do you know about his girlfriend?"

"Heather's a lawyer with a firm downtown. Zelda has had dinner with them a few times. I wasn't invited."

"Have they been going out for long?"

"For as long as I've known them."

"And how did Gladys enter the picture?"

"She was Natalie's bookkeeper."

"So Gladys has been associated with Rich for a while, then."

"I guess."

"Heather isn't Zelda's lawyer, is she?"

"No. Another firm downtown." Norman paused. "Dewey Cheatem and Howe," he said, then exploded with laughter. "It's such a stupid joke," he said, covering his mouth with his hand, "but I crack up every time I hear it."

Regan laughed. "It is a stupid joke."

"I can't remember the firm Zelda uses," Norman continued, an occasional laugh still bursting forth. "It has about six different names. You should see their letterhead. I wondered if they fight over whose name goes first."

"Maybe they take turns," Regan quipped. "I think I'll set up my laptop on the table in here."

"There's no Internet service." Norman's eyes twinkled. "You're not surprised, are you?"

"I shouldn't be."

"There's no cable, either, which is really annoying. This week I haven't been able to watch any of my favorite shows."

"This place was a real bargain," Regan commented. "I can't stop wondering who the owners are."

Norman hurried over to the counter by the back

door and rifled through his leather bag that contained mostly sheet music. "Zelda asked me to go to her apartment this morning and get the paperwork she received from the charity about this palace to show you. You want to take a look at it?"

"I more than want to take a look at it," Regan said. "Everything about this 'palace' is so curious."

19

When Zelda awoke, she stared at the ceiling, feeling groggy and overwhelmed with anxiety. She hated canceling sessions with her clients. Her father and Bobby Jo were arriving sometime tonight, and the meeting with Rich left her unnerved. She resented the condescending way he referred to her charitable donations and the help she gave her students. *Who is he to tell me what to do with my money? What did he say about investing in a vitamin company? And what did I sign?*

She reached for her cell phone, which she had silenced earlier, and tried to call Rich. It went straight to voice mail.

"Rich, this is Zelda. Could you give me a call, please? Thanks."

Then she checked her text messages. The first was from one of her students, urging her to feel better. "I wanted to tell you in person, but I can't wait, and it might cheer you up—I booked a commercial! Thanks for all your help. See you soon." The second text was from another student who told her to get well and that he was looking forward to seeing her next week. The final text was from a client she had seen just the day before. He wasn't feeling well either and said he'd be happy to reschedule at her convenience.

Griff isn't feeling well! She'd had lunch with him at the mall yesterday. Could they blame their stomach problems on the restaurant? Zelda dialed his number.

"Hey, Zelda," he said. His voice sounded so weak.

"Griff, you're sick too?" she croaked.

"Am I ever! Oh, man."

"I was trying to figure out what I ate that made me sick and was wondering if it was the cheesesteak I had for lunch at the mall. But you were the healthy one and had a salad."

Griff groaned. "You think it was the cheesesteak? It probably was."

"What do you mean? I watched you eat your salad."

"When I was at the counter getting our food, the cook made fun of me when he realized I was the one having the salad. There was some extra cheesesteak on the grill and he gave me a sample. I scarfed it down. It was delicious. Ohhhh boy."

"I'm so relieved!"

"You're relieved that I'm sick?"

"No! Of course not. I just was hoping that I didn't serve any food last night that was tainted."

"Gotcha. How was your party?"

"It was fun." Zelda glanced at the shopping bags she'd brought up to the room yesterday. "I guess you don't need your new clothes today."

"No," he said. "That's definite. I can't move."

"Give a call if you want to stop by over the weekend. Otherwise I'll see you next week."

"Okay. Thanks again for everything. I promise I'll pay you back."

Zelda smiled. "I know you will."

"I'm really lucky I met you. You've made such a difference in my life."

"Thanks, Griff. I appreciate that."

"Ciao."

"Don't say that!" Zelda cried. "Chow made us sick!"

They both chuckled as they hung up.

You see, Rich, Zelda thought, that's why I help people. Griff is truly grateful for what I do for him. And he's going to make it as an actor, I just know it. She checked her voice mail and found a message from her father. As she listened, she wrinkled her nose. Bobby Jo's the one who wants to go out to dinner when they get here, not Dad. Maybe by then I'll feel better. I have to. It's going to take fortitude to make it through the weekend.

She started to sit up, then noticed a piece of paper on the bed. Regan is here! Of course she is, it's nearly 1:00. Zelda called Regan's phone.

"Zelda!" Regan answered. "You're awake."

"Yes, but I feel light-headed. Are you here at the house?"

"In the kitchen with Norman. I'll be right up."

20

In an abandoned warehouse north of Los Angeles, a production crew was building sets for four nonunion commercials that would start filming at 6:00 P.M. The commercials were all for one product. Victorious Vitamins.

The director was tense and bedraggled. "How do you expect to make these commercials with so little money?" he'd asked the producers more than once in the last two days. There was something about them that he didn't trust.

But at the moment the director had a more pressing problem. Two actors had called to cancel this morning. One of them had landed an audition with Steven Spielberg for late this afternoon and the other was in a play downtown and realized that she'd never make it back to the theater in time. Sitting at his computer, looking at headshots, he knew there was no time to audition anyone. He'd have to hire actors based on their photos. And how many times do these actors look nothing like their picture?

He scrolled through the photos. He needed an older woman and a girl in her twenties. A snapshot of a petite white-haired woman with a great smile caught his eye. There was something about her expression that made him think she'd be exactly right for this commercial, even though she obviously wasn't a professional. "My name is Ava, but please get in touch with Maggie Keene at this number."

He picked up his phone and dialed.

A young woman answered. "Hello, this is Maggie."

"Hi, Maggie. My name is Frank Bird. I'm directing a commercial for a vitamin company and I was sent a picture of a woman named Ava."

"Yes," Maggie answered, excited but not surprised that Gladys was getting a call for an audition before she did. She had given Gladys an alias just in case Gladys wasn't thrilled that Maggie had sent her picture to God knows who.

"Are you her agent?"

"No." Maggie tried not to sound dejected. "Actually, I'm Ava's friend but I'm an actress as well. I sent in both our photos for your commercial."

"Really. What is your name?"

"Maggie Keene."

"Can you send me your photo again this minute?"

"Of course."

A moment later Frank was looking at Maggie's smiling face. She's not exactly the type I was looking for. "You have an interesting look," he said, his voice neutral.

Interesting look, Maggie thought. I hate that. "Uh-huh," she answered.

"To be truthful," he began.

Here we go, Maggie mused. He's going to tell me I'm not right and ask if Ava's available.

"I put that casting notice in this morning as a just-in-case. The parts had already been cast, but now they're open again."

Must be some project, Maggie thought.

"If you and Ava are available tonight, we can use you both. The studio is off the 405 about thirty miles north of LA."

"Tonight? You could use us both?"

"Yes. It's a vitamin for all ages. The fact that you know each other and have a relationship is great."

"I can definitely do it. Let me get in touch with Ava. If you give me your number, I'll call you right back."

"Sure."

Maggie took the number, then dialed her old friend Gladys as fast as she could. Gladys was working at her home in Burbank.

"Hello. Gladys Books Bookkeeping."

"Gladys, hi, it's Maggie from last night."

"Oh, hello, Maggie. I didn't expect to hear from you so soon."

"I felt like we connected. What are you doing tonight?"

"No particular plans." She laughed. "It's actually

126

my birthday. A friend was going to take me to dinner but her husband doesn't feel well. He's a hypochondriac if you ask me. He should just take his vitamins and stop complaining! Oh, I shouldn't say that."

Perfect!, Maggie thought. "How about if I take you out to dinner?"

"Oh, you don't have to do that."

"I want to. We'll celebrate your birthday and talk about acting."

"I don't think I'd be any good," Gladys said humbly.

"Yes, you would. Please let me take you out. My life is so unpredictable, spur of the moment plans work better for me. Come on. You can't be alone on your birthday."

"Well, sure. Why not? Where do you want to go?"

"I have a place in mind but I want it to be a surprise. How about if I pick you up at five?"

Gladys laughed. "If you insist."

"I insist. What's your address?" Maggie jotted it down. "See you at five." Quickly she called back the director. "Frank? This is Maggie Keene. Ava and I are all set for tonight."

"Great. Can you both wear something red?"

"Something red?" Maggie stammered.

"Yes. I want the scene to be vibrant, energetic."

"Right."

"These vitamins release energy."

"They sound wonderful."

"Yes, they are. I'd also like you to bring a very pale outfit. Something that looks washed out. I want to show the transformation you make after you take these vitamins."

"Of course you do. No problem. See you tonight." Maggie hung up. This is getting expensive, she thought. But I can't risk telling Gladys and having her say no. Maggie dialed her again.

"Maggie?"

"Yes, it's me. It's not your birthday if you don't open a present."

"I don't want you to get me any present," Gladys protested. "Taking me out to dinner is enough."

"No, I thought of something you're going to love. It's not expensive, but it's so cute."

"No, Maggie."

"Gladys, what size are you?"

"Petite four."

21

Petunia was bent over, applying polish to a client's toenails. Usually Imogene liked to gossip but today she was wrapped up in a romance novel. She'd been sniffling and blowing her nose for the last twenty minutes. I hope she washes her hands before I do her manicure.

"Yes, run to him," Imogene whispered, as she turned a page and read the final paragraph. Shaking her head, she closed the book and held it over her heart.

"Did it end nice?" Petunia asked, never looking up.

"Well," Imogene began, her voice choked with emotion. She paused and dabbed her eyes. "The heroine fell in love with a rich, handsome man. But he turned out to be a terrible, terrible cheat. What he put her through!"

"Aw, he ran around with other women, huh? What a shame."

"No! He cheated on his taxes!"

No big deal, Petunia thought. The IRS must think my clients are cheapskates. If I declare half my tips, they should consider themselves lucky. "It would be difficult," she said slowly, "but I'd do my best to forgive my husband if he did such a terrible thing." Concentrating hard, she inspected each toe for wayward polish. Any she found was wiped away with a sharpened stick that could easily cause pain. "I'd try to find forgiveness in my heart."

"He didn't just cheat on his taxes! He set up phony businesses all over the country. He was a scam artist. That's how he made his money."

Petunia's ears perked up. "What kind of scams?"

"It's hard to explain."

"Can I borrow the book?"

"Certainly." Imogene unzipped her large pocketbook. "A lot of his shenanigans took place on the Internet. I won't tell you the ending."

"Just tell me if he went to prison."

"No. He never got caught."

"I'll read it tonight."

Imogene sighed. "I love to read." She pulled another book from her bag. "Next up is the latest by Nora Regan Reilly."

Petunia looked up quickly. "I have a signed—" she started to say, then cut herself off by turning away and pretending to sneeze. "I sssheww! I sshewww! Oh, dear, excuse me."

"I thought you were going to say you had a signed copy."

"Where would I get a signed copy?"

"Beats me. The book is brand new."

Petunia twisted the cap on a bottle of nail polish and placed it back on her supply cart. "Ready for your manicure. Do you have to use the ladies' room first?"

"No."

"Are you sure?"

"Yes."

"Okay. Be careful stepping down from that chair."

"I feel rude for not chatting with you but I had to finish that book," Imogene said, reaching for Petunia's hand.

Petunia had no choice. "Let me help you."

Imogene squeezed Petunia's fingers as she stepped down from her perch. "And how are your girls?"

"Fine, thanks," Petunia answered, then began rolling her cart toward the front of the salon.

Imogene followed, struggling to keep her feet from falling out of paper slippers wide enough for an elephant's hoof.

"My girls both work so hard to help the underprivileged in one way or another," Petunia said when they reached her station. "I don't know where they get that urge. Must be a recessive gene that goes back to the Dark Ages."

Imogene laughed. "Don't be so hard on yourself. You have other talents." She glanced around, then whispered. "For one, you're the best manicurist I've ever had. The best!"

Petunia waved her hand. "Imogene, stop."

"I'm dead serious! Before I forget, let me give

you that book." She reached into her purse. "As a matter of fact, you can keep it."

"Really?"

Imogene nodded as she pressed the book into Petunia's hands. Together they looked down at the cover.

A drop-dead gorgeous man was rushing through an airport bare-chested, his laptop under his arm. *The Chiseled Chiseler.* "He's certainly on the go," Petunia observed. "Thank you very, very much."

"You're welcome very, very much."

This time it was Petunia who held the book close to her heart. "Your kind gesture means the world to me. You have no idea."

"I think I do. Reading something we love can have a powerful effect on our lives."

Petunia smiled. That's exactly what I'm hoping.

22

On Friday morning, high-ranking police officers from around the country gathered in the auditorium of the Los Angeles Police Department headquarters. Speakers who were experts on bank robberies, art theft, and kidnapping shared their knowledge about the latest developments in fighting and solving those crimes. Everyone was on their own for lunch and instructed to be back by 1:30.

Jack and several of his comrades walked a few blocks to a casual restaurant that was known for great hamburgers. The place was packed with workers from offices nearby and they were lucky to find a table for five. The patrons were relaxed and talking loudly, clearly excited that the weekend was about to begin.

When Jack's group was seated, they quickly placed their orders, then started to unwind.

Sergeant Derek Wentley, who lived in San Diego, leaned forward. "Jack, when they were talking about kidnapping this morning it reminded me of how you met your wife. I still can't get over that."

The others laughed. They all knew the story.

"One of the perks of the job," Jack said, enjoying the friendly banter with his comrades.

Angela Cruz, one of the highest-ranking female officers in LA, put down her water glass. "I had to go online to find my husband! When guys hear you're a cop they get nervous."

"If anyone can handle you, Victor can," Jack observed.

"Have you and Regan decided yet where you're going this weekend?" Angela asked.

"Actually, we haven't."

"No rush," she retorted.

Jack smiled. "We'll get in our rental car tomorrow morning and either go north or south."

"Hey, speaking of rental cars, did you hear about the luxury car rental business that went under?" Derek asked, not waiting for an answer. "They were renting out Bentleys and Ferraris. Problem is, car thieves showed them fake ID, used fake credit cards, and drove off with wheels worth hundreds of thousands of dollars. Never to be seen again."

"I bet they knew which way they were going," Angela said. "Right to a seaport and onto a waiting ship. Those cars were sailing across the sea in no time flat."

"There's great technology now to protect people from car theft," Jack observed, "but it doesn't work if you hand over the keys. Or leave the car running. A couple of years ago we had a rash of car thefts in New York during a brutally cold winter. Everyone turned on their cars in the morning to warm them up, then headed back into the house. For most people, that was fine, but not on the South Fork of Long Island. When many Long Islanders stepped back out, well. . . ." Jack made a face.

"Were they caught?"

"Yes. A group of college kids got cocky about stealing cars because it seemed so easy. One of them became violent when the cops showed up at his dorm to arrest him. He was an honors student on scholarship. Car theft is bad enough, but a further investigation revealed he was dealing a lot of hard drugs."

"I'm not surprised he got violent," Angela said. "When he was arrested, he was terrified that big old light shining on him was about to get brighter. But once you're in the spotlight, baby, that's it. And people who've got a lot to lose are the scariest. They'll do anything to make sure that spotlight doesn't come near them. And I mean anything."

"Thank you, Sergeant Cruz," Derek quipped. "Our next speaker who will tell us something we've never heard of is—"

Angela cackled. "Sorry. I know you know. But we just had a case where a guy went after a woman he was afraid was going to blow his cover. She knew too much. It was bad. That's all I'll say. B A D."

The waitress arrived with their food. As she was

serving, Jack tried to push back an uneasy feeling about Regan. He always worried about her, especially since her job was to find truths about people they didn't want uncovered. But the sudden realization that he knew nothing about this old friend she'd stayed with made him tense. And he hadn't even heard her voice today. I'll call her right after we get out of here, Jack thought. Everything will be fine. And as of tonight, it'll be just the two of us.

But he still couldn't shake the nagging sense that somehow that wasn't going to happen.

23

"I'm sorry," Zelda said when Regan walked back into the room. "I fell back asleep. Feeling this way is awful, but I think I know what caused it. I spoke to the client I had lunch with yesterday. He's sick, too. We both had cheesesteak."

"I guess that's good news," Regan said. "I'm glad you slept. Norman and I chatted. I told him I dropped off the knife at the police department."

"You did!"

"Yes, on my way here. Zelda, it's important to keep your door locked."

"I promise we will."

"Norman showed me the papers he picked up at your apartment regarding the charity and this house." Regan sat in the chair by the bed. "There's no information on-line about *Healthy, Healthier, Healthiest.* I did a search on my iPad and couldn't find anything."

"It's a new charity, but still, it should be listed somewhere! Could that mean it's a fake?"

"Not necessarily; but it's odd. We don't have to talk about that now. I know you want to focus on Bobby Jo."

"I do, but if *Healthy, Healthier, Healthiest* isn't legitimate, I want to know what's going on. Who are the people running it? Where is the money going? And how did they get this house for the silent auction?"

Regan took a notebook and pen out of her purse. "Let's start at the beginning. When was the first time you heard about the charity?"

"August. I received a letter in the mail inviting me to a kickoff for an exciting new charity that was set up to donate money for medical research on nutrition. The cocktail party was the Thursday after Labor Day. I remember because I already had plans. A friend of mine was in a play and it was opening night. But the play didn't start until eight o'clock. I thought I'd buy a ticket to the cocktail party and stop by when it started. I did that and only stayed fifteen minutes. Just enough time to place a bid for this house."

"Where was the party?"

"In an old building on a side street, near Santa Monica. It was a big open space. Not glamorous in the least."

"Were many people there?"

Zelda shook her head. "There were two young girls at the door with a list of names. Inside a handful of people were standing together deep in conversation. I went over to the bar and ordered a club soda. I tried to make small talk with the bartender but he was still setting up. So I busied myself looking at the silent auction items."

"Did you talk to anyone else?"

"Not really. When I was reading about each

item, a young girl who was probably in her early twenties was also checking them out. She said that she would have loved to bid on this house, but the minimum was a thousand dollars and she couldn't afford it. I remembered those days well, and thought, now I can afford it! And it's for a good cause. So I put my name down for a grand. I also bid on dinner at a couple of restaurants. Then I'd had enough of all that socializing, and I left. The next day I was shocked to get the call that I'd won the house."

"Who called you?"

"A woman named Melanie. She was really nice and thanked me profusely. She said they are trying very hard to get the charity off the ground but it's difficult because there are so many good causes for people to choose from. She asked if this week would work for me to use the house and I said yes. I knew it was around the time of my father's birthday and thought maybe he'd want to come down to celebrate by staying in a mansion in the Hollywood Hills. Huh! By this time, Bobby Jo was glued to his side and I figured she'd come along as well. But she thought a trip for two to Vegas would be more exciting. A trip I end up paying for. Lucky me. I don't see my father on his birthday, and she's still coming to the house."

"Did you speak to Melanie again?"

"No. She e-mailed me and sent the keys. They arrived the day before I was coming here."

"Didn't someone meet you here to show you around?"

Zelda shook her head.

"You just showed up and put the key in the door?"

"Yes. Thank God I have Norman."

"It's crazy. What if these people, whoever they are, accuse you of taking a painting or an antique that they claim is missing after you leave that wasn't here when you arrived?"

Zelda looked at her. "Does anything around here look like it's worth stealing?"

Regan laughed. "No, but still. There's such a thing as a walk-through. When you check out of a hotel they want to know if you took a candy bar from the minibar since the last time they inspected it."

"I'm such an idiot," Zelda said.

"No, you're not," Regan said firmly. "But now that you have deep pockets you have to be careful."

"I hope in the end I'll be glad I struck it rich," Zelda said, with a sense of foreboding.

"Of course you will," Regan said. "Your life has changed dramatically. It takes getting used to."

"I wouldn't have had these problems if I'd won the twenty-five thousand dollars on *Puzzling Words*. That money would have thrilled me and I could have handled it. It would have made my life better in a much simpler way."

"Zelda! You're going to be fine. You know what? I bet this house belongs to a long-lost cousin of someone involved in the charity who was probably too embarrassed to be here when you walked in."

"And saw the expression on my face."

"I'm sure there's a simple explanation. The people who worked on the event were probably trying to think of anything that would make money. You know, this place could really be beautiful. It's just neglected."

"I'm glad I didn't have to hop on a plane to get here. It wasn't much trouble to drive up the hill."

Regan nodded. "Don't laugh. There are stories about people who pay in advance to rent a villa somewhere exotic, and when they get there it doesn't exist. Or the place is nothing like the pictures they were shown."

Zelda opened her arms. "Like this."

"Yes."

"There wasn't a single picture of this house at that auction. What is wrong with me?"

"Nothing!" Regan said. "Enough of that." She turned the page of her notebook and poised her pen. "Tell me everything you know about Bobby Jo."

24

As time passed, he became increasingly agitated. His palms were sweating and his head was throbbing. He'd been relieved when she came out of the hotel alone, then followed her at a safe distance. When she pulled into the police station he thought he would lose his mind. He parked on a side street with a view of her car, and waited, frantically wondering what she was doing there. When she came back out, escorted by a cop, he held his breath. They opened her trunk and the cop lifted something out that glinted in the sun. He was too far away to be sure, but the way the cop handled it made him believe it was his knife! I have to check the woods. But I can't now.

He'd followed her from the police station and was in for another jolt. When she turned into the dead-end street where she'd been last night, he knew he couldn't follow her. So he parked on the canyon road and waited, his thoughts racing.

Why did she go back to that house? Why can't she go somewhere where I can get to her?

If it was my knife in her trunk, how did she find it? My fingerprints are all over the handle! I only left it in the woods because I couldn't walk to my car at daybreak carrying a knife. I should have brought a bag with me so I didn't have to leave it there.That was stupid. I waited for her all night and then I had to leave. She would have seen me.

Did she take a walk through the woods this morning? Who does she think she is? Little Red Riding Hood?

Why did she go back to that house so fast?

That knife has my fingerprints!, he kept thinking.

He reached under the seat to reassure himself that his other knife was there. "Ow," he grunted. Quickly he pulled his hand away. He stared at his index finger, transfixed by the blood spilling from the cut. "Little Red Riding Hood," he whispered. "That's who you'll be. And I'm the Big Bad Wolf."

25

Norman appeared in the doorway of Zelda's room. "Can I get either of you anything?"

"No, thanks," Regan answered.

"I have my water," Zelda informed him. "That's all I'm drinking." Then she informed him about her conversation with Griff.

"Too late, I just threw out all the food."

"Better safe than sorry. Why don't you sit down? I was about to start telling Regan about Bobby Jo."

Norman rolled his eyes. "My favorite topic." He pulled the hassock Regan had rested her feet on all night to the other side of the bed, next to where she was sitting.

"Thanks, Norman," Zelda said. "Now I can look at you both at once. It hurts to move my head, and I feel dizzy again."

"Always at your service, my dear."

Zelda smiled. "I really don't know what I'd do without you." She looked at Regan. "Norman is going to sing professionally. I can't wait for that to happen but I'll miss spending so much time with him. And I'll never find anyone as dedicated."

"Zelda!" Norman gasped. "How embarrassing! On so many levels!"

"Why is it embarrassing?" Zelda asked evenly.

"First, I never said I'm *going* to sing professionally. I said I wanted to *try* to be a singer."

"If you don't believe, then it won't happen. You have to visualize yourself as a successful singer, and declare your intentions to the world. Regan understands that."

"Of course I do," Regan interjected. "I thought I noticed sheet music in your bag. I say, go for it!"

Norman raised an eyebrow, then moved his shoulders from side to side. "I am." He pointed to his boss. "Zelda is so generous. This morning she offered to pay for my singing lessons."

"It will be my best investment ever," Zelda pronounced, then suddenly looked worried.

"Are you sure?" Norman asked. "Right after you said that you looked like you were going to be sick again."

"I'm sorry. Speaking of an investment made me think of Rich. I'm waiting for him to call me back. I don't know why he hasn't. This morning he had me sign something but I was so groggy I didn't read it. I think it was about investing in a vitamin company."

"A vitamin company?" Regan asked.

"Yes," Zelda said meekly.

"What vitamin company?"

"I don't know."

"How much did he want you to invest?"

"I don't know that either. I told you I'm an idiot."

"No, you're not. But if you weren't feeling well, and were groggy, he shouldn't have pushed you to sign anything. It could have waited."

"Rich said he was going away for the weekend and if I wanted to get in on the deal, it had to be today."

Regan's heart skipped a beat. "Zelda, using those tactics is never good. All of a sudden he has an investment for you that you've never heard of, and you have to sign on the dotted line immediately?"

Norman's jaw had dropped. "I know nothing about investments, but that fails the smell test!"

Zelda's eyes widened. Her hand flew to her chest. "You're both scaring me."

"I don't mean to scare you," Regan said.

"Me neither," Norman quickly added.

"It might be a perfectly fine investment," Regan said. "What else has he done with your money?"

Zelda squeezed her eyes shut. "I'm not really sure."

Oh boy, Regan thought. I hate to ask, but I have to. "Zelda, do you look at your account statements when they arrive?"

"Well, I glance at them when they come in. But I never take the time to study the transactions." She shook her head. "I didn't want to admit it, but Rich has been acting kind of strange lately. He seems so distracted whenever I call him. I can hear him typing at his computer. And I don't think it has anything to do with me. I was so tired a few minutes ago. Now I feel as if I've been hit by a stun gun. My heart is racing!"

Norman jumped up. "Zelda, have some water." He reached over Regan and grabbed the glass next to the bed.

Zelda turned on her side, pushed herself up, and leaned on her elbow. "Thanks," she said, taking the glass in her hand. Slowly she took her first sip.

"Are you okay?" Norman asked, sounding frightened.

Zelda nodded. "Yes. I am. Honestly. Please. Sit."

Norman obeyed. "Do you want me to roll over?"

Zelda started to choke. "Norman!" she protested. "Are you trying to kill me? The water's coming out of my nose."

"I'm trying to defuse tension."

"I know, but don't make me laugh when I've got water going down my throat."

Norman took the glass from her.

Regan was grinning as she reached for the flowered cardboard tissue box on the night stand. These two would always be friends no matter what turns their lives might take. She pulled out the last tissue and handed it to Zelda. "The box is empty."

"I'll get another," Norman said, running into the bathroom.

Regan lifted the empty box off the nightstand. A plastic coffee stirrer was right behind where the box had been, the end of the stirrer resting in a few drops of liquid. A damp ring was on the wood. Zelda was always careful about making sure her water glass went back on the coaster, Regan had observed. And she wouldn't place a stirrer on the wood, even if this furniture had seen better days. Did Rich bring in a cup of coffee with him today? If he did, he's not very considerate. I just hope that's his biggest flaw.

"Here's a new box," Norman said.

Regan pulled out a tissue, and leaned over toward the nightstand.

"Did my water glass do that?" Zelda fretted.

Regan stopped and turned to Zelda. "I don't think so. This stirrer was wet," she said, holding it up. "Did Rich bring a cup of coffee in with him today?"

"No, he brought me a cup of tea from the health food store. He said it was good for upset stomachs. It tasted awful so I only had a couple of sips." Zelda stopped, her face registering shock. "Regan, do you think he put something in that tea to make me groggy?" she asked, her voice getting higher with each word, "so that I'd *sign that paper?* I was feeling better before I drank that tea."

It's certainly possible, Regan thought.

26

Maggie parked her car and walked into Tracy's, a moderately priced department store. She passed the makeup counters, dodging all the saleswomen who were dying to have her try their brand of lipstick, perfume, eye shadow, you name it. The store wasn't too busy. She took the elevator to the second floor.

They must be wondering why I'm walking into the petite section, Maggie thought as she made her way to the sale rack. What I do for my career is ridiculous. She started rifling through the hangers in the size four section.

"Can I help you?" a woman asked, her glasses dangling from a silver chain around her neck.

"I need a red outfit, and a pale outfit, in petite four. It goes without saying that it's not for me."

"Tell me about the person you're shopping for."

I've only met her once, Maggie thought. "She's fairly conservative and is about seventy years old."

"Hmm. We have a lovely red dress that I'm sure she'll love."

Maggie watched as the saleswoman scurried away from the sale rack as though it were radioactive. Uh-oh. I might have taken on more than I can afford. I should have just asked Gladys if she'd like to be in the commercial. She probably has a red dress in her closet. A pale one, too.

As she waited, Maggie resumed looking through the sale items. It wasn't hard to understand why they hadn't been snatched up. Patterns that were nauseating, styles that looked uncomfortable. On the very last hanger was a droopy pale gray pantsuit marked down to $59.99. Perfect. Maggie lifted it off the rack.

If Gladys comes out tonight wearing something suitable for the commercial, at least I'll be able to return one of the outfits I buy. No matter how much she needed the money, Maggie would never return clothes that were gently worn. A girl in her acting class bought designer outfits whenever she had an audition for a part that called for them, and returned the clothes afterward. Maggie always prayed that someday a price tag would pop out during an audition, hopefully in front of a big-time director.

"Isn't this darling?" the saleswoman asked as she approached, holding up a red dress with thin white piping around the collar, and buttons down the front.

"That's beautiful," Maggie said truthfully. "How much is it?"

"Let me see," the woman said, putting on her glasses and checking the tag. "Three hundred and fifty-nine dollars."

"No can do."

"That's the only red outfit we have in the store that is petite four."

"I'll have to look somewhere else," Maggie said, "but I'll take this." She held up the gray pantsuit.

The saleswoman could barely hide her disdain. "Is this woman you're shopping for a friend of yours?"

Maggie crossed two fingers and held them up. "We're like this."

After she paid, Maggie hurried downstairs, making a wide berth around the makeup section. I have to hurry, she thought. There isn't much time to find a nice red outfit in petite four. Maybe I should try one of those upscale thrift shops.

At her car, Maggie reached into her purse for her keys and suddenly panicked. My makeup bag isn't here! she realized. I left it at that party last night. I had it in the bathroom off the kitchen so I could powder my nose. I didn't notice this morning because I ran out to shop au naturel.

Maggie's skin was very sensitive, so she brought her own makeup to shoots. It was specially ordered, and not available in department stores. Every other brand she tried caused her skin to flare up.

Quickly she unlocked the door and got in the car. She pulled out her phone and searched for Norman's number. I hope he doesn't have an attitude. I hope someone will be at that crazy house so I can run over there. Heck, I hope he answers the phone! She found the number and dialed. After several rings his voice mail picked up.

"Hi, it's Norman. Leave me an interesting message."

"Hi, Norman, it's Maggie, one of the waitresses from last night. I realized that I left my makeup bag in the bathroom off the kitchen. I really need it. Are you or Zelda there today? Could I please stop by? Thanks so much. My number is. . . ."

After she hung up, Maggie was a wreck. I shouldn't have been such a wise guy to Norman last night. I hope he doesn't act spiteful and delay calling back. Maggie started the car. If Norman doesn't call back soon, I'll just go over to the house.

What's the worst that can happen?

27

"Zelda, take it easy!" Regan urged. She put her hands on Zelda's shoulders to calm her. "We'll have that liquid on the nightstand tested if necessary."

"All of a sudden it feels like everything is crashing down on me!" Tears spilled from Zelda's eyes. "My whole world has been turned upside down," she sobbed.

"I know," Regan said. "But we'll set it right."

"How?" Zelda demanded, wiping her eyes.

"We'll have your statements examined and if we find anything questionable, I'll do a background check on Rich. We can always find someone else to handle your money."

"What about Bobby Jo?" Zelda asked wearily. "I'm stuck with her. The worst part is, I feel as if I've lost my father."

"We'll find out everything we can about her, too," Regan said. "If she's okay, then we'll have to pray that she grows on you."

"I honestly don't think that's going to happen."

Regan sighed. "That's a tough one, Zelda. But your father doesn't sound like someone who would let your relationship with him suffer. I remember all the stories you told me about your parents when we were at the game show. Your father loves you."

"And so do your friends!" Norman interjected.

"That's right," Regan agreed. "The ones I met last night were terrific. And before long I just know you'll meet the right person who will complete your life."

Zelda sniffled. "I have a better chance of being left another eight million dollars."

"Whoever thought it would happen once?" Regan asked.

Norman patted Zelda's back. "Everything will be okay."

"I don't know why I'm overreacting. I coach people on how to handle the problems in their lives, and look at me. If my clients could see me now, they'd never come back."

"Are you kidding?" Norman asked. "You don't even charge some of them. And you told me just this morning that you help them in other ways. They should be thrilled to have you as a coach."

"I bought one of my clients lunch yesterday and we both ended up with food poisoning."

"That's not your fault," Regan said.

"I know," Zelda sniffled. "And I did buy him clothes that he really needed for some auditions."

"Now it's time to let people help you," Regan said. "Why don't we start by taking a quick look at your financial statements? Hopefully that will put your mind at ease."

Zelda wiped her eyes. "Okay. But they're at my apartment."

"Do you want me to go get them?" Regan asked.

"I'll go," Norman offered. "It won't take long."

Regan looked at him. "Are you sure? If you have things to do around here—"

"I'm sure. I know where everything is."

"It would be helpful if you brought back any papers or documents that Rich had anything to do with," Regan said. "That includes e-mail and legal documents."

"Okay."

"Zelda, do you have a will?" Regan asked.

"Yes, I told Rich today that I wanted to change it because of Bobby Jo."

"Norman, bring that back, too."

"It's in the safe," Zelda told him. "The key is in a little green purse hanging on a hook in my bedroom closet. You can't miss it."

"I'll return shortly," Norman assured them.

"Stop at a drugstore and see if you can pick up a small glass bottle with a tiny eyedropper," Regan instructed. "We need something like that to collect the tea on the nightstand."

"No problem." Norman hurried out of the room.

Regan sat down. "Zelda, we haven't talked about Gladys. She pays your bills?"

"Yes. Everything that isn't automatically charged to my credit card."

"What else does she do for you?"

"She does my taxes. I don't make a lot of money coaching but she keeps track of all that. And she enters all my expenses into a computer program called Monthly Math. At the press of a button I can find out how much I spent so far this year on things like my maintenance or my mortgage or find out how much I donated to charity. It's helpful at tax time."

"I've heard of other programs similar to that, but not Monthly Math. We should tell Norman to be sure and bring back that paperwork."

"I don't have any yet," Zelda said. "I received the money last November. Gladys started me on the program at the beginning of this year. She said she'd give me the full accounting when the year ends."

"But Zelda," Regan said. "It's called Monthly Math. She should be sending you a monthly statement, shouldn't she?"

"I never thought of that until now. But sometimes when I'm on the phone with her I ask how much I've spent on whatever, or how much I've made from my business. She always gives me an amount that sounds right. Should I call her and ask her to e-mail me what she has so far for this year? Norman can print it out at my apartment."

"Don't call her yet," Regan said. "Let's see what the statements from Rich look like first. Norman told me that you met Rich and Gladys after Florence Natalie died and that they had worked for her."

"Yes."

"How long did you know Florence?"

"We were neighbors for almost ten years."

"And you never saw Rich or Gladys in your building?"

"No. I never saw anyone going in or out of Florence's apartment except Florence and her dog. He was her constant companion. She told me she liked to take him on long walks whenever she had the energy."

"We'll figure this out," Regan said. She looked at the drops of tea on the nightstand. "Let's not wait until Norman gets back to do something with that liquid. Just in case we have to test it. I don't think we will. You don't have a little bottle, do you?"

"No."

"Let me go downstairs and take a look around the kitchen. Why don't you try and close your eyes."

"I will." Zelda reached for Regan's hand. "I can't thank you enough. If you weren't here, I don't know what I would do."

"I'm glad to help in any way I can, Zelda." Regan left the room and hurried downstairs. She was walking across the living room when her cell phone rang. It was Jack. Thank God, she thought. I came down just in time.

28

Norman grabbed his beeping phone off the kitchen counter and raced out of the house. When he was in his car, he quickly checked for messages. Someone had called from a number he didn't recognize. Forget it, he thought, tossing his phone on the seat, I'll deal with it later. He started the car and backed down the driveway. At the end of the street he waited until the coast was clear so he could pull out and turn left.

There was so much traffic. They should put a light here, he thought. But they won't spend the money on a street with only one house that no one lives in. Finally there was an opening Norman thought he could make. He pressed on the gas, screeched forward, and hung a left.

Zelda lived in a new complex in the hills just north of Sunset Boulevard. He was there in fifteen minutes. Once inside her bright, comfortable apartment, with its beautiful views of Los Angeles, he headed to her bedroom closet and found the key to the safe in the green purse. He hurried down the hall to Zelda's office and opened the door into the walk-in closet. He put the key in the large safe, opened it, and looked inside. Stuffed to the gills, he thought. I only wish I needed a safe. He removed several jewelry cases, Zelda's passport, her birth certificate. On the bottom he saw a manila envelope:

LAST WILL AND TESTAMENT OF ZELDA ALICE HORN

This gives me the creeps! Norman thought. He removed the envelope, returned everything else, closed the door, and locked the safe. He placed the will on Zelda's desk and put the key back in the green pocketbook. In the hall closet, he found a small suitcase. Back in the office he opened the suitcase on the floor and started looking through the file cabinet. He found the account statements and tossed them in the suitcase, followed by files on Florence Natalie, Zelda's clients, and her father. Regan told me to bring back anything that might be relevant, Norman thought. It all seems relevant! Zelda talked to Rich about everything going on in her life.

Finally Norman finished. He grabbed the will and tossed it on top of the other papers, zipped the valise, and wheeled it to the front door.

Anything else I should take care of while I'm here? he wondered.

See if she has any messages. Most people call her cell phone, but still. He went over to the answering machine in the living room. The light was flashing. He pressed play.

"Zelda, this is Rich. Wait, I called your home phone by mistake. Sorry."

What a genius, Norman thought.

The next message was from Los Angeles Sunny . . .

The message stopped. "Your mailbox is full," the machine announced. Three beeps followed.

"Zelda!" Norman gasped. "You have to erase old messages." He pressed play. The machine announced that there were twenty-eight messages, and started to replay them. Most were from Rich, telling Zelda to give him a call. Norman listened, taking brief notes on a pad by the phone. He deleted the messages he knew Zelda absolutely didn't need; they dated back a month. She should let me clear her machine once in a while, Norman thought. I'm ruthless with the delete button.

"Hey, Zelda . . ."

Rich's voice again, Norman thought with disgust.

"I thought I'd catch you. You must have left for your stay at the Scrumps estate. I hope you enjoy it. I'll call you on your cell. Bye."

Before the message disconnected, Norman heard Rich mumble something and laugh. What was he saying? Norman played the message again, his ear cocked over the speaker of the machine. After Rich's words about the Scrumps estate ended, there was a few seconds of dead air, then Rich sounded like he wasn't near the phone when he sarcastically mumbled, "Wait until she—" and laughed. A high-pitched beep signaling that the message had ended made Norman jump.

"Wait until she what?" Norman shouted. "I knew from day one you were no good!" Impatiently, he listened to the rest of the messages. A moment later he was out in the hall waiting for the elevator, Zelda's suitcase by his side. I have to find an eyedropper fast, he thought, pressing the elevator button again and again. Zelda was so upset about everything, and she had a right to be, but it was more than that. He'd never seen her cry like that. She'd once told him that she had two teeth pulled when she was in college. They gave her a drug that put her to sleep and she woke up sobbing.

There was no doubt in Norman's mind that Rich had laced Zelda's tea. Why else would she have reacted like that today?

29

"Jack!" Regan said as she answered her phone and walked into the kitchen. "I really hope we don't get disconnected. The cell phone service in this house is unreliable."

"I miss you. All of a sudden it seems like forever since I've seen you."

"I feel the same way."

"Your text said you were going back to your friend Zelda's?" he asked.

"Yes." Regan explained to him Zelda's concerns about her financial adviser and her stepmother. "We're trying to get things straightened out."

"But you're okay."

"Yes, of course I am. Jack, I hope I won't be delayed in getting back for dinner tonight. I don't know how long this will take."

"Don't worry about it. If you're delayed, I'll come over to Zelda's. Give me the address."

Regan smiled. Jack never complains or makes me feel guilty. "I don't know why I was lucky enough to find you," she said after giving him directions to the Scrumps estate.

"You were born under a lucky star," Jack joked. "But so was I."

"How's your day been?"

"Interesting. We're a much bigger group today. It's good to reconnect with people I haven't seen for a while. A few of us had lunch together at a restaurant near headquarters. We're heading back to the auditorium for the afternoon session in a few minutes. I'll call you when we finish and see what's up."

Should I tell him about my visit to a police station this morning? Regan wondered. No. He sounds too worried. The problem is that when Jack gets a feeling about something, he's usually right. Regan teased that she was going to buy him a crystal ball.

"Regan, are you there?"

"Yes, of course."

"If you need any help finding information about these people, you know you can call my office."

"Thanks, Jack. I love you."

"I love you, too. Be careful."

"I will."

When Regan hung up the phone, she stood quietly for a moment. I can't wait to see him, she thought. It won't be long. She glanced around the kitchen wondering what went on in the house when people actually lived here. There must be some clues somewhere. She shrugged. I can't think about that now. There are more important issues to deal with.

She found a small glass bowl, brought it

163

upstairs, and placed it upside down over the liquid on the dresser. Zelda was in the bathroom.

Regan sat down with her iPad and entered Rich's name into a search engine.

30

In the auditorium at LAPD headquarters, Jack's lunch buddies were saving him a seat. He headed down the aisle, saying hello to people he knew along the way.

"Hey, Jack, how's it going?"

"Great. You?"

"Can't complain."

"Jack, good to see you."

"You, too."

The program was about to begin. The final stragglers were wandering in. On the stage, the microphone was being tested.

Jack was about to take his seat when he felt a tap on his shoulder. He turned around. An officer from the LAPD introduced himself.

"I wanted to say hello. My name is Lew Martin. I met your wife several years ago when we arrested a guy she investigated. She's terrific."

"Thanks," Jack said. "I agree."

"I just heard she's working overtime. We could use her back in Los Angeles, but thanks to you we lost her to New York." Martin laughed.

Jack smiled. "Overtime?"

Martin leaned in and lowered his voice. "I hear that knife she found in the woods is a beauty."

Jack raised his eyebrows slightly, an expression

that was meant to convey disbelief at the situation, not that he was hearing this for the first time.

"Tell her the guys at the precinct over in Hollywood are grateful she dropped it off this morning. More patrols have been ordered. A knife like that, hidden in the woods near hiking trails?"

An announcement was made from the podium: "Could everyone please be seated?"

"Good to meet you, Jack. Say hello to Regan for me."

Jack barely heard him.

31

Two crew members on the Victorious Vitamins shoot were working together on the set for one of the ads. Their commercial would feature a couch potato couple who develop an amazing love for exercise and healthy food after four weeks of ingesting the vitamins. In the first scene the pair sits on the couch eating giant bowls of ice cream and watching television. Opened bags of potato chips, candy bars, French fries, doughnuts, cakes, cookies, and bottles of soda are scattered on the coffee table in front of them.

Four quick scenes follow.

First we see the couple taking the vitamins for one week. Some of the junk food has been thrown into a clear trash can next to the coffee table. The couple looks a little more alive. The next scene takes place after they have taken Victorious Vitamins for two weeks. More junk food has been discarded and the twosome is sitting up straight and starting to smile. In the third scene the couple is wearing exercise clothing and all the junk food has been cleared from the table. In the final scene the energetic duo is laughing and cheering as they jog around the couch, weights in their hands. The trash can is gone. Fruits and vegetables cover every inch of the coffee table.

"Hey, Ernie," one of the crew said. "This plastic window we're supposed to hang on the wall behind the couch is cracked and broken."

Ernie shrugged as he sawed a piece of plywood. "I've never been on such a shoddy project in my life. Max, you think these vitamins are for real?"

"Nah. If I thought the vitamins would cut down on the number of doughnuts I eat, I might try them. But what they're claiming is impossible. Besides, I like my donuts. I eat my vegetables, too, but I don't run around the couch cheering about them."

"If the company fails they should sell the commercials to a comedy station. I can't wait until the actors get here and start rehearsing. How they do this stuff with straight faces is beyond me."

In the back room of the warehouse, Rich and Heather, producers of the commercial, were meeting with the director, Frank Bird. Frank had asked for the meeting. He was clearly upset.

"You're not spending enough money," Frank complained. "The sets are cheesy. I'd like to rent furniture to use in the scenes. I checked, and there's a company not far from here that has what we need."

"I'm sorry," Rich said, shaking his head. "We've spent a great deal of money developing the product and we have to keep our costs down. This is only the beginning. Once orders start pouring in, we'll have money to spend on advertising.

Don't forget, the commercials we're doing today cost money to put on the air."

"Who developed this product?" Frank asked.

"We're working with a brilliant scientist."

"Named?"

"The person wishes to remain anonymous."

Frank frowned. "I can't understand why. Do you have FDA approval?"

Heather leaned forward and cleared her throat. "Food supplements do not require FDA approval."

"That's great. Okay. I hope the reason you're not spending money today is because you spent it all developing a safe, healthy product."

"Without question we have a product that is safe, healthy, and effective," Heather replied. "We're confident Victorious Vitamins will procure a large percentage of the market."

"Right," Frank said, wishing he could just walk away from the job and never see these people again. "One more question."

"Yes?" Rich asked.

"I was hired Wednesday night. What happened to your original director?"

"We didn't feel he was capable," Rich answered, his jaw tight. "We saw your reel and knew you were the one who would convey our vision for Victorious Vitamins—pep, energy, health—"

Frank stood. "I'll do the best I can. But don't

blame me if these commercials are embarrassing. I just hope the actors are decent. I'm not the one who chose most of them." He looked the two of them in the eye. "I'm forty-two years old. I got into this business late in life because I decided I wanted to do something I love, something I can be proud of. I hope your vitamins are as good as you say they are."

He walked out of the room and shut the door.

32

Maggie went to two thrift shops that weren't well stocked with petites, never mind anything red in a petite four. Then it struck her. She was wasting precious time. Thrift shops only can sell what people donate. They don't place orders. It's hit or miss. What she was looking for would not be easily obtained in a used clothing store.

Sitting in her car in front of I'll Have Seconds, Maggie got up the nerve to call Gladys. She knew it was her only hope.

"Hi, Maggie," Gladys answered cheerfully. "My size hasn't changed since we last spoke." She laughed. "I'm looking forward to tonight."

"Me too. Funny you mention your size," Maggie said, her voice casual. "The restaurant just sent me an e-mail confirming our reservation. They're trying out theme nights. Tonight they suggest people wear red. I don't know. Does that grab you?"

"A theme night? This isn't a raucous, noisy place, is it? I'd like to see you but I can't hear myself think when—"

"Oh, no!" Maggie said quickly. "It's elegant. You'll love it. Do you have a red outfit?"

"Yes."

"Do you have any problem wearing it tonight?"

"No. I'll wear red. Sounds like fun."

"Atta girl. See you later."

Maggie hung up the phone and breathed a sigh of relief. What's wrong with me? I should have made that call a few hours ago. Now I'll buy Gladys a box of candy so she'll have something to open. If the only package I have for her is that gray pantsuit she might throw it at me. I wouldn't blame her.

Norman hadn't called back yet. I know he's doing that to annoy me, she thought. If he wants me to beg, I'll beg. She dialed his number. Naturally, he didn't answer. "Norman, please, I'm begging you to call me back. It's important." Then she sent him a text that started with the word EMERGENCY.

That should get his attention, she thought. Now to the chocolate shop. I could drive there in my sleep.

33

Norman was determined to find a glass bottle with an eyedropper top but he wasn't having much luck. He'd gone to three different drugstores. There must be someplace nearby that has one, he thought. I want to save every last drop of that tea. It's living proof that Rich drugged Zelda! He'll pay for this. I hope he rots in prison for the rest of his life!

What else is he capable of?

Norman steered his car into another crowded parking lot and started looking for a space. All this in and out of the car is so stressful, and I've got to get back to the house. Regan and Zelda are waiting for that suitcase.

Rich was never very nice to me, Norman thought resentfully. What was his problem? What did I ever do to him? I never mentioned my feelings to Zelda because she seemed happy with him. Now I'm ready to dish!

Norman's phone rang. He found a space, pulled in, then looked at his phone. Is that the same number that came up before? I think it is. I can't get involved in a conversation right now.

He got out of the car and ran into a drugstore. They had what he was looking for, but the line at the checkout was long. As he waited, he knew that precious minutes were being wasted.

But this is important, he told himself, the tiny bottle in his hand.

We must preserve the evidence.

Evidence of bodily harm.

34

In the den of her home in Summit, New Jersey, Nora Regan Reilly turned on the evening news. She was waiting for her husband Luke, owner of three funeral homes, to return from work. They'd have a drink, then go to dinner at a cozy Italian restaurant in town. Tomorrow afternoon Nora had a signing at a local bookstore for her new release. She enjoyed seeing people who came back every year and now felt like old friends. It would be a pleasant weekend.

I wonder how Regan is doing, Nora thought as she sat on the couch. I hope everything works out for poor Zelda. Come to think of it . . . Nora got up and walked over to the cabinet under the television. She pulled open a drawer, found the DVD of *Puzzling Words*, and popped it in the DVD player.

She sat back down, a remote control in hand. Boy, would Regan give me grief if she walked in now, Nora thought. I'm only playing this because I'd like to see Zelda again. She fast forwarded past Regan's appearance, hard as it was not to stop and watch Regan's killer expression when she lost the bonus round. But Luke would be home soon and he'd seen this more than once.

There she is. Nora watched as Zelda was introduced. She looked so friendly with that cherubic smile. Her long curly hair was pulled off her face with jeweled combs. A green and white peasant blouse and silver jewelry flattered her coloring.

"My name is Zelda Horn and I'm from Santa Maria."

Nora watched the entire game. Zelda was so excited when she won, grabbing the elbow of the actor she played with, her expression stunned.

Time for the big-money bonus round.

I know what's coming, Nora thought, and it's not good. Zelda looked so hopeful and bright-eyed when the round began. She had one minute to guess ten words. But it was as if the actor she was playing with suddenly took a dummy pill. He blanked out. "Uhhh," he said more than once, "uhhhh." What was his problem? Nora wondered. Zelda was a good player but had no chance. The look on her face when the round ended could break your heart. She even patted that dummy's hand and said not to worry, trying hard to be a good sport.

Nora laughed out loud. Not my Regan. She didn't come close to patting her celebrity's hand. It looked more like she wanted to bite it. But in fairness, Regan would have won that money so easily if it weren't for the horrible clue on the last word. Nora shut off the DVD.

Thinking about Regan reminded Nora of the letter she had started to tell her about earlier in the day.

What was it about that request? Nora went upstairs to her office and found the file she kept on books sent to charity. She brought the letter back downstairs, poured a glass of wine, and sat at the kitchen table.

The letter was written on 8 1/2 x 11 paper with flowers bordering the sides. "Dear Nora" was handwritten. The body of the letter was typed. It began "Hello, my name is Chris Clare." She then wrote about doing good works for children and how her volunteering made a difference. Nothing specific. She stated that Nora was one of 100 people *chosen* to receive this letter. That's a good one, Nora thought. I really didn't look at this closely before. Here's something! At the beginning of the note, the woman says her name is Chris Clare, then signs it Clare Chris. What a doozy! And of course I sent the book to a PO box.

I'd love to see where that book is now.

The back door opened. Luke stepped into the kitchen and walked over to the table. "Hello, my dear," he said, leaning over and giving Nora a kiss.

"Hello. Glad you're home."

"Me too. What are you reading?"

"A letter I was telling Regan about today. Requesting a book. I'm sure that whoever sent it isn't doing all the good deeds she claims to be doing. Let me get you a glass of wine."

Luke took off his coat and hung it in the hall closet. "How is our daughter?"

"She ran into a young woman—Zelda—who she met when she did that game show. Zelda's father got married at a drive-through chapel in Las Vegas the other day to someone he hasn't known long. She asked Regan to see what she could dig up on the new bride."

"Not a bad idea," Luke said as they walked into the den together. "Though I hope Regan and Jack are able to enjoy their weekend."

"I hope so, too. But you know Regan. She'll never walk away from someone who asks for her help."

"That's what always worries me."

35

At first glance, Regan couldn't find much about Rich Willowwood or Richard Willowwood online. She did find a site that listed Rich's business, Willowwood Management in Sherman Oaks. Investment services with a staff of one to four and a Web address. She entered the URL and was told the website was under construction. No other information was available.

Zelda came out of the bathroom. "I'd like to take a shower, but I think I'll go back to bed for a few minutes."

"A shower?" Regan asked. "Can you stand for that long?"

"I don't know. I'll go back to bed and decide. Regan, you look tired."

"I'm okay."

"You slept in the chair all night. Why don't you go into one of the bedrooms and close your eyes for a few minutes? You have plans with Jack tonight. I don't want you to be exhausted. Norman will probably be back soon with those statements. Give yourself a breather."

"You don't want to talk about Bobby Jo?"

Zelda shook her head. "I can't think about her at the moment. She's coming here, ready or not. We'll worry about her later. Rich, on the other hand, I can worry about as soon as Norman returns." Zelda got back into bed and sighed. "Please, Regan. Why don't you rest for a few minutes?"

Regan put her hand on the back of her neck. "Maybe I will stretch out. Sometimes when I try to take a nap I just stare at the ceiling. But I use the time thinking."

"So go think," Zelda said. "And I hope you rest."

Regan went into the bedroom downstairs where the coats had been kept for the party. This is really not a bad house, she thought. It's just dated. The room didn't get much light. Heavy drapes nearly covered windows that faced the backyard. Somber, dark furniture added to the feeling of gloom, but the room had a certain old-fashioned smell that Regan didn't mind.

She took off her shoes, pulled back the flowered spread, and laid down. The bed was surprisingly comfortable. Her body was grateful to rest on a flat surface. The house was quiet and peaceful and she dozed off within minutes.

When Regan awoke she blinked her eyes. Once again, it took her a moment to acclimate. She looked at her watch and was surprised to see that it was 2:45. She had slept for an hour. Didn't Norman get back yet? she wondered. Feeling slightly chilled, she rubbed her arms, then got up. She put the bedspread back in place, then pulled on her boots. She turned her head at the sound of a creak in the hallway. "Norman?" she called.

No answer.

She walked to the door and glanced down the hall. The air was still and quiet. Regan sighed. I must have heard one of those creaky old house noises. But you don't have to be in an old house to hear those sounds, she reminded herself. Regan had a friend in New York who lived in a brand-new, narrow high-rise building by the East River. When the wind kicked up, the apartment creaked like a cruise ship. Regan turned, walked over to the bathroom, and pulled open the door.

Look at this! The walls were all mirrored, covered with heavy beveled glass, much of it cracked. An old-fashioned claw-foot tub was to the left, a toilet to the right. Regan flicked on the light, then stepped toward the sink. I do look tired, she thought.

Her eyes widened.

Behind her, a tall male figure stepped into the doorway, a knife raised over his head. Regan screamed as he lunged toward her. She dodged to the left, scampering over the tub, desperately looking for a way to escape.

He fell toward the sink. "Shut up!" he yelled.

She grabbed the long dangling silver hose hanging over the faucet of the tub and swung it like a baseball bat toward the creep she'd seen in the mall parking lot who was lunging at her. The rusty nozzle at the end of the hose smacked him in the face. He grabbed the cord and flung it against the glass wall.

That's it, Regan thought frantically. I'm finished. She backed into the corner, screaming bloody murder. It was too late. There was no way out. Blood was dripping from his nose. He was coming toward her again.

Suddenly he howled as a glass tile hit the back of his head and crashed to the floor. He slumped over the tub, lost his grip on the knife, and moaned in pain.

Zelda was standing behind him in her nightgown.

"Zelda!" Regan grabbed the knife from the tub. "We don't have much time." They darted out of the bathroom and shut the door. "This dresser!" Regan ordered. Together they pushed the heavy piece of furniture until it completely blocked the door. Regan picked up the knife and pointed the blade toward the floor. "We have to get out of here!" She took Zelda's hand and ran with her down the hallway and through the kitchen. Regan grabbed her car keys, and they raced outside.

Norman was coming up the driveway.

"Call 911!" Regan screamed. "Now!"

36

A long-winded speaker was taking questions when an LAPD officer appeared next to Jack's seat. He leaned down. Jack looked up at him.

"Everything's okay, but your wife just called," the officer whispered.

Jack didn't wait for an explanation. He bolted out of his seat and hurried up the aisle. Outside the auditorium an LAPD police car was waiting. Jack sprinted toward it and jumped in. The car sped off, its siren blaring.

37

Regan and Zelda were sitting with Norman in his car at the bottom of the driveway, the engine running in case Regan's attacker emerged from the house.

Norman had called 911 then Regan phoned Jack and LAPD headquarters downtown so Jack would get word of what happened immediately.

"Before all hell breaks loose, tell me what happened!" Norman gasped.

"A lunatic came up behind me in that mirrored bathroom and tried to stab me," Regan said, still gasping for breath. She dropped the knife on the floor of Norman's car. "This looks exactly like the one I found in the woods."

"Oh, my God!"

"Zelda came to my rescue," she added quickly.

"How?" Norman cried.

"I heard Regan scream and I raced downstairs. I'd noticed a loose glass tile in that bathroom the first day we arrived," Zelda explained. "It was leaning against the wall next to the door. I grabbed it and whacked him in the head."

"Zelda, I'm so proud of you!" Norman said, grabbing her hand. "Who was this guy?"

Regan and Zelda started speaking at once. They looked at each other. Zelda looked distressed.

"What's the matter, Zelda?" Regan asked. "You saved my life."

"But it's my fault."

"What are you talking about?"

"That lunatic was my client."

"What?" Regan asked, shocked.

"Client? Which one?" Norman demanded.

"Griff!"

"Griff!" Norman echoed. "Griff?"

"Yes," Zelda answered. "I should have known. I played right into his hands."

"What do you mean?" Regan asked.

"When I first met with him six months ago, he told me all about his problems. His home life hadn't been great. His father split when he was twelve, and his mother was left with three kids. She did her best, but she worked long hours at a menial job. There wasn't much money. Griff told me he hung with the wrong crowd in high school and got in a lot of trouble. A couple years after he graduated, he came to L.A. to try to make it as an actor. He said he'd wanted to put the past behind him and make something of himself. But by the time I met him, he was twenty-four, hadn't had much success, and was really discouraged. Money was a problem. I told him he didn't have to pay me right away. We'd work together, and when he started to do well, he could pay me."

"Zelda, that's commendable," Regan said.

"But Regan, now it's clear he was out to use me

from the beginning! I met him when I went to see a client I was helping out who was in a showcase with Griff. When I congratulated Griff on his performance, he seemed so vulnerable and unsure of himself. I told him to call me. Griff came to me knowing exactly how to manipulate me so I'd spend money on him. Which I did! I've paid his rent for months now. Yesterday, I bought him lunch. He whined that he didn't have the right clothes to wear to auditions, so I took him shopping for clothes. Then he complained his car had a flat tire and he had to ride his bicycle to the mall. He probably wanted me to buy him a new tire! I took his clothes home with me because I bought him so much stuff he couldn't carry the bags on his bicycle. He was supposed to pick them up today but we both got sick. He didn't look sick to me! Physically, that is." Zelda covered her face. "I feel so stupid. Any doubts I had, I ignored. I should have cut him off three months ago. But what made him come to the house? Why did he attack you? What was he going to do next?"

"Zelda, it's my fault."

"Your fault? Why?"

"After you pulled out of your parking spot at the mall, I was standing there when he emerged from a stairwell," Regan began, then quickly told about her encounter with Griff.

"You think he was trying to steal a car?" Zelda asked.

"It sure looked that way."

"Wait a minute!" Zelda said. "Yesterday I couldn't find my ticket to get out of the garage. Griff offered to hold my purse when I went into the dressing room for two minutes to try on a pair of pants. He was so sweet and grateful that I'd shopped for him. I bet he rifled through my purse and took the ticket!"

"It makes sense," Regan said. "If he had a ticket, it would be much easier for him to drive out with a stolen car."

"But if he realized you were watching him yesterday, he probably didn't steal a car. So why would he want to harm you?"

"There must be something else he wants to hide," Regan said. "We'll find out."

Norman looked woeful. "When I ran out to get the statements, I was in such a rush. I pulled the door behind me, but didn't make sure it was completely shut. That must be how he got in the house."

"Don't worry about it, Norman," Regan said. "Now this nut is off the streets. He won't have a chance to harm anyone else. If he was capable of doing this to me, he is certainly capable of doing it to someone else."

"You're right, Regan," Norman said. He pointed his finger. "You are absolutely right! And that's what I say about Rich Willowwood or Woodwillow or whatever his name is. If he was capable of putting drugs in Zelda's tea, which I'm *sure* he did, then what else is he capable of?"

"What if I had been too groggy to hear Regan scream?" Zelda asked angrily.

Regan grabbed Zelda's hand. "We still have work to do."

Sirens pierced the air. Two police cars came racing down the block, their lights flashing. Norman followed them up the driveway and jumped out of the car.

"The intruder was armed and dangerous!" he yelled. "Armed and dangerous! I'll unlock the door!"

Norman's phone began blaring a Broadway show tune. Regan reached for it as Zelda got out of the car. Could it be? she wondered. Yes. She answered.

When she heard Jack's voice, she started to cry.

38

Please let someone be there, Maggie prayed as she turned off the canyon road and onto the Scrumps estate's block. Please please pretty please.

She drove around the bend, turned into the driveway, and started up the hill. What's going on here? she wondered.

Three police cars were parked near the house, their lights flashing, their radios squawking. A guy in handcuffs was being led out of the house.

He wasn't at the party last night, Maggie thought. I hope everyone is okay. Even Norman. I'd better stay out of the way. She pulled over onto what once must have been a lawn. She had no idea what to call it now. Wait till I tell them that I'm only here to pick up my makeup. That's going to sound really swift. She stopped the car and got out.

An officer came over to her.

"Hi," Maggie said. "Is everything okay?"

He nodded, clearly not wishing to converse. "Do you know these people?" he asked, nodding toward the house.

"I worked at a party here last night. I left something behind."

"I'm sorry," he said. "You'll have to come back later."

Maggie shook her head. "You don't understand. It's my makeup and I'm an actress. Tonight I'm shooting a commercial—"

"This is a crime scene."

Regan had just hung up with Jack. When she saw Maggie looking distressed she hurried over. "It's okay," Regan said to the officer, "I'll talk to her."

"Oh, thank you. We met last night. My name is Maggie Keene."

"I'm Regan Reilly."

"What happened?" Maggie asked, aghast.

"That guy getting into the police car tried to kill me."

Maggie looked stunned. "Why?"

"We're going to find out. I'm a private investigator."

"I'm really sorry," Maggie said. "I'm really happy you're okay. That sounds trite. Obviously I'm glad." All of a sudden she felt very flustered.

"I understand," Regan said. "What can I help you with?"

"Now this really sounds stupid. I left my makeup bag in the bathroom off the kitchen. I'm an actress and I have a commercial shoot tonight. I'm allergic to the makeup they use at shoots."

"I know all about allergies. Listen, it's a good thing you didn't leave the makeup in the bathroom where the coats were kept last night. That's where he tried to attack me. That room probably has yellow crime scene tape across the doorway."

"That mirrored room?"

"Yes."

"Whew. Okay, then. That place already looked like a crime scene."

Regan laughed. "Wait here."

"Thank you. I really appreciate it."

A few minutes later Regan returned. "This is cute," she said, holding up the makeup bag decorated with four leaf clovers. "I guess you're Irish, too."

"Yes. From Chicago. My little niece gave me this. She hoped it would bring me good luck with my acting."

"I hope it does, too. Something brought me good luck today, that's for sure," Regan said.

"Definitely. Thanks again," Maggie said sincerely. "If there's anything I can ever do for you, anything, please let me know." She gave Regan her card. "If you ever have a party, I'll work for free."

Regan laughed. "I live in New York."

"You never know. You never know when our paths might cross again."

"That's true. Well, have a good shoot. What's the commercial for, anyway?"

"Some kind of vitamins. I'm sure the commercial's going to be really lame. I can just tell."

"What vitamins?" Regan asked quickly.

"Victorious Vitamins. Can you believe that name? They're brand new and supposed to be super-duper for people of all ages. Give me a break. But, hey, it's a job."

"Where's the shoot?"

"Thirty miles north of here. I'd better get going. I have to get ready and get up there."

"Maggie," Regan said. "This could be a long-shot. But I might need your help sooner than you think."

"Really? Sure. What?"

"Zelda's financial adviser, Rich, talked to her about a new vitamin company this morning and she agreed to invest. She's a little concerned now that it might be a little too risky for her tastes. There are so many products out there that claim to be bigger, better—"

"I know! Years ago my parents got talked into putting money in a company that claimed they were reinventing the pressure cooker. Forget it. It's like reinventing the wheel. Pointless. My parents laugh about it now, especially since the guy who took their money is in jail. In my family, as long as you get a story out of something, it's worth it."

Sounds like my family, Regan thought. "Maggie, I wonder if you would keep your ear to the ground at the shoot, and see what you can find out about the vitamin company. It might be the same company. Probably not, but Rich said something about a vitamin for all ages."

Maggie stared at Regan.

"What?" Regan asked.

"This is going to sound strange."

"Try me."

"I got friendly with Gladys the bookkeeper last night."

"And?"

"Well, we snapped a few pictures."

"Yes." I'm afraid to hear what's coming, Regan thought.

"Gladys told me she had always wanted to be an actress. Today I was looking at the auditions posted online and I sent in Gladys's picture to a couple different places. Wouldn't you know, I got a call a few minutes later and we were both cast for the commercial. We didn't have to audition. See what I mean? They must be desperate."

"Gladys is in the commercial?" Regan asked.

"She will be."

"Oh. Then it probably isn't the same company. Gladys works with Zelda's adviser."

"Gladys doesn't know she's going to be in the commercial. It's a surprise. She thinks we're going out to dinner. I thought she'd be so thrilled to finally get a chance to act."

"Oh," Regan said. "I'll bet she'll be surprised."

"If Rich only mentioned the investment to Zelda today, Gladys might not know yet, right?" Maggie said practically. "I'd imagine he doesn't consult with Gladys about investments."

"Probably not. Maggie, please do me a favor. Don't mention our concern to Gladys."

"Of course not!"

"I probably shouldn't have mentioned anything about it. I'm just trying to help Zelda out."

"Regan, don't forget about the Keene family pressure cooker investment! I understand. My lips are sealed. Give me your number. I'll call you from the shoot and tell you what's happening."

"Great. Call me on my cell. I hope it goes well."

"Thanks. We'll see!" Maggie got in her car, started the engine, and waved goodbye.

She's a nice girl, Regan thought. But I never should have opened my mouth.

39

Inside the house, Norman was busy spreading the account statements out on the dining room table. I can't believe I missed all the excitement. If I'd been here, maybe I could have tripped him or something. But as Regan said, Griff's off the streets now. Next we have to get Rich off the money, then off the streets. And anyone else who has their eyes on Zelda's loot.

The police were questioning Zelda and Regan in the living room.

Norman looked out the window. A patrol car was coming up the driveway. Another one? A guy got out the back and hurried toward the side door. I bet that's Regan's husband.

"Regan," he called, not caring whether he interrupted the questioning. "I think your husband is here."

"Thank you."

Regan excused herself from the living room, and hurried through the kitchen. Norman peeked around the corner as Regan and Jack flew into each other's arms next to the ugly pink stove. Jack lifted Regan off the ground and kissed her, then cradled her head to his chest tenderly, looking like he'd never let go.

"I love you," Jack said.

"I love you, too. All I could think of was that I'd never see you again."

I'm going to cry, Norman thought. I really am. When am I going to find love like that? The same time Zelda does. Never. Back to the statements.

A little before five, Frank was checking all the sets, anxious for the first actors to arrive at the warehouse. They were due in a few minutes.

I just don't trust those producers, Frank thought. If I were casting for corrupt characters, those two wouldn't have to audition. All of a sudden they seem nervous. I told them to grab some dinner and come back later, but they're sticking around.

When I escape this place tonight, I'll want to celebrate. But I'll probably just head home.

At the other end of the room, two actors came through the door, carrying hanging bags and looking lost.

"Hello," Frank called, walking toward them. "Welcome. We've got a changing room. I'd love to get a look at your wardrobe. . . ."

Heather and Rich were in the back office. Rich finished a call.

"Did the money get wired out?" Heather asked.

"Not yet," Rich said. He looked at his phone. "Zelda sent another text."

After the police left, Zelda took a shower, which made her feel more human, while Regan and Jack collected the drops of tea on the nightstand.

"Let's hope we don't need to test this," Jack said quietly as he twisted the cap on the bottle. He hugged Regan. "We don't need any more trouble."

Norman was still sorting papers. When he finished putting everything in order, the four of them began to review Zelda's statements together.

It didn't take long for the situation to become upsetting.

Rich had set up three different accounts for Zelda. When they started looking at the monthly statements, they realized that regular wire transfers had started in January, two months after Zelda received the $8 million. The money had been wired to different banks, but Zelda had no idea what the transfers were for. With each passing month the amount wired out increased.

"He must have been testing the waters," Zelda said incredulously, "to see if I was paying attention. I wasn't, so the transfers started getting larger."

"Did you sign anything that gave Rich authority to make these withdrawals?" Jack asked.

"Not that I remember. I signed a lot of papers. I didn't always read the fine print. It's my fault. I trusted Rich. He told me that I should focus on getting my business off the ground and spend my time doing what I do best. Coaching. He'd worry about my finances."

Regan hit the table with her palm. "Another ruse! Con men like Rich say that all the time, especially to people in the arts. Whenever someone handling your money feeds you that line, run as fast as you can in the other direction. What they're really saying is, 'Do what you do best while I do what I do best—rip you off.'"

Zelda looked frightened. "Wow, Regan."

"I'm sorry to upset you. But it's true."

"I'd better freeze my accounts this minute."

"Let's do it," Jack agreed.

When Zelda got on the phone with the bank, she was told that a $2 million transfer was in the works.

"What?" Zelda shrieked. "No! I want that canceled immediately!"

Jack took the phone, identified himself, and asked to speak to a bank officer, who assured him that the transaction was canceled. He told the officer not to give any information to Rich Willowwood, who would be notified that he was no longer Zelda Horn's financial advisor. Zelda faxed a letter to the bank with the same information. She tried to call Rich for an explanation, and sent him a text, but he didn't respond.

"What do we do now?" Zelda asked anxiously.

"At least he no longer has access to your money," Regan said, trying to reassure her.

"But looking at those statements . . . we haven't added everything up but he already transferred several hundred thousand dollars."

"We'll get a forensic accountant to find out exactly where that money went," Regan said. "Hopefully Rich put some of the money into investments you're not aware of."

Zelda shook her head. "I doubt it. I can't believe this is happening. If I get my hands on him—"

"His office is in Sherman Oaks?" Jack asked, looking down at a statement. "Have you ever been there?"

"No."

"Where does he live?"

"Santa Monica. I don't even have the address. Last year I wanted to send him a Christmas card and he told me to send it to the office. In the back of my mind it always bothered me that he wouldn't give me his address. Should I call Gladys and ask if she knows anything about these transfers?"

"You might not reach her," Regan said, then added, "Gladys is shooting a commercial tonight."

"What?" Zelda asked.

Regan told them about her conversation with Maggie.

"Gladys is in a commercial for a vitamin company?" Norman asked, incredulous.

"I know what you're thinking," Regan said. "It does seem funny given the timing of Zelda's investment. But Maggie's the one who sent in Gladys's photo. Gladys thinks she's being taken out for a birthday dinner."

Zelda looked at Regan. "A birthday dinner? I feel terrible. I didn't realize it's her birthday. That's a good reason to call her." Zelda picked up her phone and dialed Gladys's number. No answer. She left a message. "Hi, Gladys. It's Zelda. Happy birthday! I should have had a cake for you at the party last night. Call me when you can. Bye."

"How sweet," Norman muttered.

"Now what?" Zelda asked. "This is devastating. I can't figure out how he expected to get away with withdrawing two million dollars from my account. Was it *all* going into the vitamin company? This is just unbelievable! I don't care if I signed a piece of paper or not!"

Norman pointed to the glass bottle containing the drops of tea. "Hmmm. Rich knew you usually signed papers without really studying them, but he couldn't take the chance you'd really read them this time. He had to make sure you were a little out of it."

"But why now? I'd realize pretty quickly the money was gone. Two million dollars is twenty-five percent of all my money! I would never have put that much in one investment."

"Zelda, it's Friday night," Jack said. "Nothing more can be done about the wire transfers until Monday. But I can call my office now and ask them to start checking Rich's background."

"That would be great. Thank you. I'd hate to have to wait until Monday to keep going with this." She smiled wistfully. "It's going to be a long weekend anyway."

"I heard," Jack said sympathetically. "Regan told me. That situation with your father's wife might turn out okay. But if you'd like, I can have my office start looking into her background as well."

Zelda hesitated. "I feel so guilty about it now. What happened to Regan today could have been tragic. Rich wiring money out of my accounts is terrible on a completely different level. Obviously. Those things are so much worse than being upset about who my father married. Bobby Jo is his wife. I can't have you do that."

"You can't stand her," Norman reminded Zelda. "And don't forget they got married at a drive-through chapel sitting in the back of a cab!"

He does speak his mind, Regan thought.

"Okay, then." Zelda sighed. "But only because Norman would never let me hear the end of it if I said no."

"Perfect!" Norman cried, patting Zelda's arm. "Jack, I'll write down that information for you."

"Thanks," Jack said, following him into the kitchen.

"It seems like ages ago we were on that game show, doesn't it?"

"A lifetime ago," Zelda answered sadly.

"I didn't say that to make you feel bad."

"I know you didn't."

Regan's phone rang. She picked it up and answered.

"Hello."

"Regan, it's Maggie!"

"Oh, hi, Maggie."

Zelda sat up in her chair.

"I'm at the shoot," Maggie whispered. "Gladys seemed surprised when we pulled up to the warehouse but she thanked me for what I'd done. The minute we walked in the door she told me she had to use the bathroom. I decided I might as well, too, and followed a few steps behind. She went straight to a back office! Rich's girlfriend answered the door! I could see Rich sitting at a table. Isn't that weird?"

"Yes, it is," Regan answered quickly. "What's the address?" She scrawled it on a piece of paper. "We're on our way."

42

The commercial shoot wasn't going well. At the moment they were filming the couch potato couple in their final scene. No one could accuse the actor of not being committed to his work. Weights in hand, he looked jubilant as he and his TV wife ran around the couch. Seized by an actorly impulse, he turned to blow her a loving kiss, tripped, and fell to the ground. On the way down his forehead grazed the ragged corner of the plywood coffee table. Several pieces of fruit that had been borrowed from the crafts services table fell to the ground and rolled away.

"Cut!" Frank called.

Crew members rushed to the actor's aid. The thespian jumped up and started running in place. His forehead had been scraped. *"I'm fine. Perfectly fine!* Just a few splinters."

The makeup girl, armed with tweezers, removed the splinters and patted his nose with a sponge. "Good as new."

"YES, I AM!" the actor bellowed. "Ready to go."

Maggie, watching from the side, shook her head. This guy must be desperate for work. But I should talk. I make up a story to get Gladys here and have to shop for an outfit for her, just so I could act in something like this? Maggie looked around. Where is she? I know she's not thrilled to be an actress named Ava. I hope Regan and the gang arrive soon. That should be interesting.

Jack was driving Zelda's Mercedes up the 405 freeway with Regan in the passenger seat. Zelda had insisted on getting in the back with Norman.

"I'm so excited," Norman announced. "But what do we do when we get there?"

"Don't worry," Jack told him. "If Zelda were a two million dollar investor in these vitamins, she'd have a right to stop by the commercial shoot." Jack winked at Zelda in the mirror. "Right, Zelda?"

Zelda grunted. "Right."

"She also has a right to ask Rich a few questions about the company. Then we'll move on to other interesting topics."

"Like wire transfers," Regan said flippantly.

Zelda patted her bag. "The statements are right here."

"Maybe we'll follow Mr. Willowwood home tonight," Jack suggested. "See where he lives."

Norman clapped his hands. "That'd be good!"

"We're not going to let him off the hook," Jack promised, putting on the blinker and changing lanes. "Not with what he tried to pull today."

Rich and Heather were closeted in the back office at the warehouse, afraid to show their faces. Not with that girl who worked at the party last night in their midst. What bad luck to have her send in Glady's picture! How can Gladys be in the commercial? It's too dangerous. When these vitamins fail, and we know they will before long, you don't want the company bookkeeper onscreen. No. You want the business to fade away without a trace. A new venture is just around the corner.

"He hasn't called back," Rich said nervously.

"He will," Heather said, trying to sound confident.

"It's never taken this long for a wire transfer. Why didn't it go through yet?"

"There's probably a good reason."

Rich's phone rang. It was his contact at the bank, the one who always made sure things went smoothly. For a price.

"Hello," Rich said.

"I'm sorry, Rich," he said in a hushed tone. "The transfer was canceled and the bank was informed that you are no longer the financial adviser for Zelda Horn."

Rich's face crumbled.

"And I'm afraid that our friends are not going to be happy when the two million doesn't arrive. Maybe you should abandon ship."

45

After they exited the 405, Jack followed the instructions given by Zelda's GPS. Five miles later they found themselves in a remote, poorly lit industrial neighborhood.

"You have reached your destination," the GPS informed them.

"It's got to be one of these warehouses," Regan said, looking around.

To the right they saw a car pull out of the parking lot, make a right, then sail past them.

"That was Rich!" Zelda cried.

"We'll follow him." Jack stepped on the gas.

"He's going so fast!" Norman observed.

"I hope he doesn't recognize the car," Zelda said.

"We'll be okay," Jack assured her. "He's not looking back."

"Rich, oh my God!" Heather wailed. "Oh my God."

"We'll get the money we stashed, then head to the airport and get away until this blows over. It will, don't worry. We'll have the other money soon."

"I hope my parents aren't home."

"If they are, make up a story. You're good at that."

"Look who's talking."

Rich was reaching speeds that were much too dangerous to keep up with. Jack could see the car in the distance as he asked Regan to call 911. "This guy is bad enough. We don't need him crashing into a vehicle full of innocent people."

Rich sped into the driveway of his destination. Heather jumped out, keys in hand. Rich followed, leaving the car running. Heather unlocked the door and they ran into the house.

"Hi, Daddy," she said, rushing past her father. He was watching television.

"Hi," he grunted, barely noticing.

Heather swung around the corner and started down the stairs to the basement, surprised the light was on.

Her mother screamed.

"Mom, what are you doing?" Heather asked as she ran over to the bookshelf, reached for a secret latch, and pulled the unit away from the wall.

Petunia, a yellow highlighter in her hand, had been sitting at her desk reading *The Chiseled Chiseler.* "What are you doing? I didn't know we had a secret closet!"

"I had it installed before you moved in. I just have to grab a few things and we'll be on our way." Heather started stuffing cash in a bag.

I was wrong about the recessive gene, Petunia thought.

"Hello, Mrs. Hedges," Rich said as he flew by her desk. "Heather, let me help you."

"Mom, what have you got going on down here?" Heather asked as she looked around, trying to decide what else she should take with her.

"Nothing special."

There were two police cars in the driveway. Jack asked the officers to give him a minute before they went in. One of them had clocked Rich at 100 miles per hour.

Regan, Jack, Norman, and Zelda hurried up the walk. The front door of the house was wide open. Zelda knocked.

"Door's open," Clarence grunted, never taking his eyes off the baseball game. San Francisco was ahead by one run.

"Are Heather and Rich here?" Zelda asked.

"Downstairs."

"Thanks."

Zelda, Jack, Regan, and Norman filed past him, then hurried down the basement steps.

Petunia screamed again.

Rich turned and glared at Zelda. "What are you doing here?" he spat. Heather was crouched down inside a small closet. A closet that you'd never know existed. When you closed the door it disappeared behind a bookcase.

"What are *you* doing here? What were you planning to do with my two million dollars?" Zelda demanded.

Two million dollars! I'm in the wrong business, Petunia thought.

"Get out of here," Heather barked, pushing herself up. "This is private property."

"How about my property?" Zelda moved toward the closet.

Heather blocked the doorway. But she couldn't hide the row of shelves on the back of the open door, lined with neatly labeled binders. Zelda turned. "What do we have here? Oh, how interesting. Last Will and Testament of Florence Natalie. A binder with my name. A binder with Norman's name?"

Norman jumped. "What did I do?"

A book on a table caught Regan's eye. She inched closer. Other books, CDs, and autographed photos from celebrities were also neatly displayed. AUCTION ITEMS (FOR THE INTERNET!) was written in bold red letters on a piece of computer paper. Regan smiled, picked up her mother's book, and tapped Petunia on the shoulder.

"Yes," Petunia said, turning away from Zelda and Heather and Rich's argument.

"You like her books?"

"Very much."

"She's my mother."

Petunia screamed once again.

On the stairs they could hear footsteps. Two police officers appeared.

"We're here to arrest the driver of the vehicle outside that reached speeds of. . . ."

You can run, Rich, Regan thought, but you can't hide. We got you.

46

All the files and cash in the hidden closet were seized from Petunia's basement. Not her auction items, she was given a pass on that. They weren't included in the search warrant the police had obtained.

"I told Maggie we would head back to the commercial shoot," Regan said as their group got in Zelda's car. "I want to look for any evidence Rich and Heather may have left behind."

"The more evidence the better!" Norman said. "I can't wait to see them in court."

When they walked into the warehouse, Maggie came running over. She'd been on the lookout for them.

"Rich and Heather ran out the back door," she whispered excitedly. "They told the director they had an emergency. I can tell the director thinks they're jerks. And Gladys took off right after they left. She called a cab! One of the crew members did my scene with me. We're almost finished."

"Where's the office?" Regan asked.

"In the back. Follow me."

Quietly they crossed the cement floor, avoiding numerous cables and wires. In a far corner, bright lights were shining on an actor holding up a bottle of Victorious Vitamins. You're wasting your time, Regan thought.

Maggie stopped in front of the office door, slowly opened it, then flicked on the light.

The room was small, with cement block walls, a harsh overhead fluorescent light, a metal table, and four chairs. Two empty paper coffee cups had been left on the table.

"They cleared out," Regan said, "except for the cups."

"I bet we wouldn't find any trace of a sedative in those," Norman sniffed.

"OKAY, THAT'S A WRAP!"

"That's the director, Frank," Maggie told them. "He's really nice. I feel sorry for him."

"Would you introduce us?" Regan asked.

"Sure."

Frank Bird was tall and attractive, with dark hair and a boyish face. He was wearing jeans, a black T-shirt, and a baseball cap. When Maggie made the introduction he was friendly, but preoccupied, and seemed stressed out. When he heard Rich and Heather had been arrested, he became even more so. "I knew it!" he said, folding his arms across his chest. "I'm afraid that all these people won't get paid."

"One way or the other we'll make sure they do," Zelda told him.

Frank turned to her and suddenly took notice.

There's something about her, he thought. And she's so pretty.

"I want to have a wrap party at my house tomorrow night," Zelda continued. "Anyone who survived working with Rich and Heather should help celebrate their downfall."

Frank gently touched her arm. "I'll be there."

"Great. Let's get everyone's attention."

When they got back in the car, Zelda looked at her watch. "My father must have gotten to the house a while ago. I wonder how he's doing."

"We'll be there soon," Jack told her.

In the back seat, Norman was in heaven, looking out the window and envisioning Rich in a cold dank cell.

Jack had just turned off the 405 when his phone rang. It was his office. The phone wasn't programmed to Zelda's car so he pulled over to take the call.

"Hello."

"Jack, it's Tom."

"Hey, Tom. What have you got?"

"We didn't find any criminal record for either Rich Willowwood or—"

"You will soon," Jack interrupted.

"Okay," Tom said with a slight laugh. "We didn't find a criminal record on Bobby Jo Bartinger but we do have other information about her."

"Just a second, Tom." Jack turned to the others

and told them. "Okay, Tom, do you mind if I put you on speaker?"

"Not at all."

Zelda held her breath.

"After you called before, I phoned my wife at home. She loves to go on the Internet and search for information that wouldn't come up easily in a background check."

"What did she find?"

"Apparently Bobby Jo's grandfather was a notorious criminal in New Mexico, who did time for armed robbery. Time and time again I should say. He'd get out of jail and then rob another bank in six months. The family tried to distance themselves from him. They didn't want people to discover their connection to such a morally corrupt individual. It's understandable. People make snap judgments and think behavior like that is in the genes. The article my wife found was written thirty years ago for a small town paper in northern California. Bobby Jo's mother, also named Bobby Jo, was interviewed on her deathbed. She talked about her father and how hard he'd made life for the family. Young Bobby Jo was at her bedside. Her husband had just died in a tragic accident. She was quoted as saying she'd never love again."

"Wow," Jack said quietly.

"When people gave those local interviews thirty years ago, I'm sure they never expected their story would be accessible to the whole world three decades later. My wife claims that the kind of background check she does helps you understand what's really going on in a person's life."

"It's true," Jack said. "Thanks Tom. And thank your wife for us."

"Yes, definitely thank your wife," Zelda said.

When they pulled up the driveway of the Scrumps estate, Zelda's father's car came into view. Inside, they found Bobby Jo and Roger standing at the kitchen table, surrounded by food. They were laughing as they unpacked grocery bags. Bobby Jo looked up when the door opened.

"Zelda, hello!" she said with a big smile. "There was nothing in the refrigerator so I told your father we should go out grocery shopping. You people must be hungry. Let me fix you something. I hope you don't mind—"

"I don't mind at all." Zelda walked toward Bobby Jo and gave her a hug.

Saturday, October 6th

47

After a restful day, Regan and Jack got in the car and headed toward the Scrumps estate for Zelda's party. They were driving down Sunset Boulevard when Regan gasped and pointed at a billboard.

"What?" Jack asked quickly, glancing at the ad for the latest luxury car. A hip young guy with a scruffy beard and a smug expression was sitting at the wheel. "Is that Griff?"

"Yes. That ad will be coming down soon."

Earlier in the day they learned from the police that Griff confessed he had stolen cars and brought them to an illegal chop shop when he needed extra money. After his run-in with Regan at the garage, Griff watched her go to security and then followed her. He panicked when he realized that his face would soon be in a national ad campaign and Regan might identify him. He was worried that an investigation would expose him and his tough guy cohorts at the chop shop, who would surely retaliate.

At the Scrumps estate, preparations for the party were in full swing. The caterers were preparing hors d'oeuvres, except this time Maggie wasn't among them. She would be a guest tonight. Bobby Jo was helping Zelda and Norman with other last-minute details.

Zelda had asked Regan and Jack to arrive early. She'd gotten a call from the police. Investigators had already been looking through the documents that they'd taken out of Petunia's basement. There were a few important items they wanted her to see.

The detectives arrived shortly after Regan and Jack.

"Bobby Jo, would you get my father? I want him to hear the latest developments."

"Of course. I think he's about ready now."

Officers Cal Spiedel and Donald Oppelt walked into the living room with Jack and Regan, noticing a karaoke machine in the corner.

"Looks like it'll be a fun party," Cal commented.

"Here we all are," Zelda said, as she and Norman, her father, and Bobby Jo all sat down.

"We didn't want to take up too much of your time," Officer Spiedel began. "But we were sure that you'd be interested in what we have to tell you."

"We are," Zelda said.

"First off, it seems that Rich Willowwood and Heather Hedges were quite a pair of schemers. They really went to great lengths to make a buck off other people." He opened a binder. "Florence Natalie left letters with her estate papers that Rich and Heather, as her co-executors, should have given you. There's one here for you, Zelda, and one for Norman."

"Me?" Norman cried. "Me? I'm afraid to read it."

Cal smiled. "You don't have to be. Believe me." He handed them both the letters.

"Can we read them now?" Zelda asked.

"Sure."

"You go first, Norman."

"Okay." He pulled an old piece of stationery out of a plain envelope and unfolded it. Engraved on the top of the letter was a sketch of a house. "Look at this drawing," Norman said quickly. "It looks like this house."

"What does it say?" Zelda asked impatiently.

Norman cleared his throat.

Dear Norman,

I'm sorry we didn't become friends, but I'm not one for socializing anyway. After my husband died, I wanted to stay to myself. I had such a wonderful life with him and I'm happy to live with my memories.

We lived in a lovely old house on a hill where we hosted so many parties during our fifty years there. Such fun we had! We'd sing and dance and stay up until the sun rose behind the woods near our home. Then we'd have a champagne breakfast.

After my husband died I didn't want to stay there. I couldn't. It was too painful. Before I moved I kept hoping my husband would walk through the door. But I couldn't bear to sell the house, either. Sometimes I'd take my dog (I'm sorry about your groceries!) and walk up into the Hollywood Hills to my home. I'd walk through those rooms, then sit in the living room and remember all the wonderful times.

We never had children so I have to decide what to do with my earthly possessions. When I walk by your door, I sometimes hear you singing. Once I passed your door when it was open. Your apartment is so inviting and attractive.

Norman, I am happy to bequeath you my home, The Scrumps Estate . . .

Norman jumped up and screamed. "Is she kidding?"

"Keep reading!" Zelda ordered.

Norman adjusted his glasses.

and I hope you restore it to its former glory. I own all the land on the block. One or two more houses could be built without destroying the natural beauty of the surroundings. Sell a piece of land so you can afford to live there. Then put your efforts into becoming a singer. You're quite good!

Most sincerely,
Florence Natalie

P.S. You really should learn to like dogs. They're wonderful companions.

"I love dogs!" Norman screamed. "I LOVE DOGS! He took off his glasses and wiped his eyes. "This is my house. Isn't it *gorgeous?* I love it here!"

They all laughed.

"Norman, that's great!" Zelda said.

"Truly great, fabulous, terrific . . ." the others echoed.

Regan looked at the detectives. "How were Rich and Heather going to pull this off?"

"They'd forged a new will that didn't include the house, then transferred the title of the house into an LLC they created called The Scrumps Estate. But Florence's legal will was in that closet, along with these letters. Both wills were dated at the beginning of last year. Because Natalie didn't have an heir, Rich and Heather assumed that the will wouldn't be scrutinized."

Norman was mumbling to himself. "I hope they rot in prison."

"Do you know how they met Florence Natalie?" Zelda asked. "Or how long they knew her?"

"Yes, we do. Heather was very organized and kept a diary and detailed notes. Apparently Florence Natalie had made out a will after her husband died eleven years ago. She planned to leave her money to a charity that got a lot of negative publicity at the beginning of last year when a reporter discovered the executives were paying themselves huge salaries and bonuses. Florence decided she needed to change her will, but her lawyer had died. She looked in the Yellow Pages, found the name of a law firm that handled wills, and gave them a call. She was put through to Heather, who apparently decided to handle Florence's estate without involving her firm. All she needed was a little help from her boyfriend Rich. I'm sure they presented themselves as invaluable legal and financial advisors, with Florence's best interests at heart. When Natalie died six months later, Rich and Heather were the co-executors of her estate."

"She didn't have a financial adviser when she met Rich?" Jack asked.

"No. Her husband had handled their money. Before he died he had liquidated their investments. She never changed anything after that. She just paid her bills."

"What about Gladys?" Zelda asked. "Wasn't she Florence's bookkeeper?"

Spiedel shook his head. "No. Gladys had been fired by Heather's law firm for mismanagement of the books. Heather got in touch with her after she and Rich met Florence. They paid Gladys to be a witness to both versions of the will. Then they brought her in on Zelda's business dealings."

"No wonder she never wanted to talk about Florence!" Zelda said. "Whenever I brought up her name, Gladys would say it was too upsetting to talk about her dear friend. Oh! It's just unbelievable!"

"I wonder how Heather and Rich got together," Regan said.

Oppelt smiled. "According to Heather's diary, they met at a networking party two years ago."

"There you go," Regan said. "These days it's all about making connections."

"Those two must have really hit it off," Spiedel said. "It didn't take long for them to become partners in crime. With Rich's financial background and Heather's legal knowledge, they were a perfect combination. They were just getting started, but they'd already marketed several products online, including a night mask that will not only block out the light but also will remove wrinkles while you sleep. That's a good one, huh?"

Zelda was shaking her head. "Wait, this means that Rich and Heather must have donated this house for the charity auction. Why?"

"That charity, *Healthy, Healthier, Healthiest*, is run by a friend of Heather's. A former friend I should say. Heather bragged to this woman that she and her boyfriend were the executors of an estate that included a mansion in the Hollywood Hills. It was going to be sold, but Heather offered it as an auction item. She said it needed sprucing up, but she would take care of it before anyone stayed there. She never did. I spoke to the woman from the charity today, and she seemed uncomfortable about the whole thing."

"They didn't bother to freshen it up because it was me who would be staying here!" Zelda exclaimed. "And now I know for sure why no one from the charity wanted to show their face." She turned to Regan. "Can you believe this?"

Regan nodded. "Yes, I can. Zelda, why don't you read your letter?"

"I already have the money Florence left me so I don't think there will be any big surprises." Zelda looked up at the detectives. "I wonder why Rich and Heather paid me."

"They thought Florence Natalie had told you about the bequest you were receiving."

"That's a stroke of luck."

"Read your letter," Norman urged.

"Okay." Zelda pulled out the letter, written on the same stationery.

Dear Zelda,

You don't know how much it means to me that you offered to walk my dog. Anyone who's a friend of Porgie's is a friend of mine.

I can't tell you how much I enjoyed seeing you on that game show. I was so sorry you lost. It was so unfair. That actor you were playing with gave you terrible clues! You were so gracious to him after you lost out on that money. I was very impressed. I'll never forget it. The girl who was on before you looked none too pleased.

Regan raised her hand. "That's me!"

They all laughed.

Jack squeezed Regan's arm and smiled. "I wish I'd been there."

Zelda continued reading the letter.

But I must say I would have reacted the same way.

"You see!" Regan crowed. "Did she leave me any money?"

Zelda laughed. "I don't think so."

"Read the rest," Norman urged.

I'd like to leave you a gift that should add up to eight million dollars after taxes. I hope you enjoy the freedom it gives you to follow your dreams. I know you'll make a difference in this world.

Sincerely,
Florence Natalie

P.S. If you want to hear about my life, ask Norman. I wrote his letter first. Now my hand is tired.

Zelda looked up. "Wow. Who would have ever thought?"

The doorbell rang.

"We have a lot more to discover about those two," Officer Spiedel said. "But we knew that you'd want to hear what we've learned so far. Your party is starting. I have a feeling it's going to be a good one. We'll be in touch."

"It's going to be the best party ever!" Norman cried.

Frank Bird came around the corner, dressed in black, looking handsome, and decidedly less stressed than he did the night before. When he saw Zelda he smiled. "Did I arrive too early?"

Zelda's eyes shone as she got up to greet him. "Not at all. This is the perfect time."

Jack turned to Regan. "Well, my dear, we can still take off tomorrow for a couple days of vacation. We'll just have to decide whether we want to go north or south."

"With us it never matters," Regan said. "We're already there."

About the Author

New York Times bestselling author Carol Higgins Clark has written fourteen previous Regan Reilly mysteries. She is also co-author, with her mother, Mary Higgins Clark, of a bestselling holiday suspense series. Carol's first mystery, *Decked*, was published in 1992 and was nominated for both the Anthony and the Agatha Awards.

Also an actress, Carol studied at the Beverly Hills Playhouse after receiving her B.A, from Mount Holyoke College. She appeared in Wendy Wasserstein's *Uncommon Women and Others* at Carnegie Hall, a play set at Mount Holyoke. Recently she played twins who own a bar together in the TNT production of *Deck the Halls*, the first book Carol wrote with her mother. It's also the book in which Regan meets Jack.

Using one word titles ending in "ED" came about by accident. After *Decked*, Carol wrote a book about a murder at a pantyhose convention. She joked that it should be called *Snagged*. *Snagged* it was! The rest is history! Carol has a long list of titles to come.

Center Point Large Print
600 Brooks Road / PO Box 1
Thorndike ME 04986-0001 USA

(207) 568-3717

US & Canada:
1 800 929-9108
www.centerpointlargeprint.com